MODERN

Glamour. Power. Passion.

MILLS & BOON

First Published 2026
First Australian Paperback Edition 2026
ISBN 978 1 038 97450 1

MIX
Paper | Supporting responsible forestry
FSC® C001695

Published by
Harlequin Mills & Boon
An imprint of Harlequin Enterprises (Australia) Pty Limited
(ABN 47 001 180 918), a subsidiary of HarperCollins
Publishers Australia Pty Limited
(ABN 36 009 913 517)
Level 19, 201 Elizabeth Street
SYDNEY NSW 2000 AUSTRALIA

Printed and bound in Australia by McPherson's Printing Group

Out Of Office Temptation

Cathy Williams

MILLS & BOON

Books by Cathy Williams

Harlequin Modern

A Week with the Forbidden Greek
The Housekeeper's Invitation to Italy
The Italian's Innocent Cinderella
Unveiled as the Italian's Bride
Bound by Her Baby Revelation
Emergency Engagement
Snowbound Then Pregnant
Her Boss's Proposition
Billionaire's Reunion Bargain
Heir for the Holidays
Maid for the Italian

Secrets of Billionaires' Secretaries

A Wedding Negotiation with Her Boss
Royally Promoted

Visit the Author Profile page
at millsandboon.com.au for more titles.

Cathy Williams can remember reading Harlequin books as a teenager, and now that she is writing them, she remains an avid fan. For her, there is nothing like creating romantic stories and engaging plots, and each and every book is a new adventure. Cathy lives in London, and her three daughters—Charlotte, Olivia and Emma—have always been, and continue to be, the greatest inspirations in her life.

To my wonderful and inspiring daughters,
Charlotte, Olivia and Emma.

CHAPTER ONE

ERIN'S PHONE BUZZED. She didn't bother to look at it because she knew exactly who was texting her. That made it six texts since she had arrived at her boss's mansion in Chelsea, where a celebratory cocktail party was currently in full swing.

Raffaele Rossi had just closed a major deal and the champagne was flowing. The company he had acquired was small but in rude health. They needed his financial clout to take the next step and he wanted them because in under three years, he anticipated their stock skyrocketing with his judicious investment, bringing yet more millions into his already healthy coffers.

More than the money, though, Raffaele Rossi would be celebrating the new challenge of taking something small and turning it into something huge. Every new acquisition had him as excited as a kid in a candy shop.

Thirty people were milling around in his living room while waiters and waitresses circulated with trays of exquisite canapés and, naturally, the finest champagne on tap.

Lawyers, most with other halves, accountants, most with other halves, the CEOs of the firm Raffaele had taken over, *all* with other halves—and Erin. With no other half and text messages that kept coming through.

She caught Raffaele's eye across the crowded sitting room and he winked at her. Erin's mouth tightened in response, and she saw him stifling laughter.

She swiped a passing canapé and turned to one of the young lawyers next to her, a guy she had met several times over several deals. He had been trying to engage her in conversation while she distractedly banked down rising impatience with her boss. This time, she wouldn't be making her excuses early and leaving, which was her usual approach to these dos. No, she would be sticking it out, because she intended to have a word with her boss and for once, to heck with the consequences.

Enough was enough.

'Your phone seems to be buzzing again.'

'I know.' Erin smiled apologetically at Colin. He was a bit older than her, with a neat, tidy appearance that belied a sharp legal brain. She might only have met him a few times but she'd always liked what she'd seen.

'Maybe you should just answer whoever keeps trying to get in touch.'

'No. I won't be doing that, Colin.' Erin smiled at him when he reddened. 'And I don't mean to be rude. What do you think of the company merger? Are you exhausted after working solidly for the past week?'

'Comes with the fat salary, doesn't it?' He grinned. They looked at one another in a moment of wry agreement.

'That and loyalty.' Erin wondered how loyal her boss would think her once she'd given him a piece of her mind.

'Everybody knows that Rossi Holdings is the golden

ticket. Pays the most and in fairness, we only have to work mega long hours now and again. People would kill for my job so even if I was collapsing on my feet, I'd know better than to complain. What do you think the next big deal's going to be?'

'You know I can't breathe a word about what's in the pipeline.' Smiling, Erin met his eyes and made a shushing gesture with her finger over her mouth.

'What's it like working for Raffaele every day, Erin? I only deal with him when something like this happens and it's all hands to the pump. Is he as tough as everyone says?'

'Tough but fair.'

'Tough, fair and with a different woman on his arm every other week. Sorry.' Colin looked at his champagne flute ruefully. 'Too much of the fine stuff. I'm gossiping.'

Erin laughed but didn't carry the conversation further.

A different woman every other week? Maybe not quite that…but it definitely wasn't a million miles away from the truth.

She stole a look through her lashes at Raffaele, who was standing across the room. She knew very well that if he caught her eye, he would raise his eyebrows and stifle another amused grin.

He thought Erin was dull.

Dull but incredibly capable, incredibly efficient and probably indispensable. She caught a glimpse of herself in an impressive oval mirror sandwiched between two abstract paintings. Shoulder-length chestnut hair, hazel eyes, short, straight nose and full lips. Not unattractive, she knew, but definitely not in the same ballpark as the string of women who entered and exited Raffaele's life with monotonous regularity.

She suspected, in addition to *dull but incredibly capable, incredibly efficient and probably indispensable*, she could likely add *plain*.

The perfect secretary from Raffaele's point of view.

Certainly, before Erin had arrived four years ago, her boss had managed to burn his way through six PAs, all of whom, he had later confided, had to be dispatched because they'd ended up having a crush on him.

He'd confessed that he was in perpetual mourning for the sixty-something-year-old lady who'd worked for him for years before inconsiderately inconveniencing him by emigrating to New Zealand to be with her daughter and grandchildren.

Erin had stepped in, killed his curiosity about her personal life before it could really take root, and now they couldn't have had a more harmonious working relationship.

Except for the times when she'd had to grit her teeth and remind herself of the size of her pay cheque.

Like now.

Except this evening, she was going to do a little bit more than grit her teeth.

'What are you doing after this?'

'Huh?' Eric blinked and looked at Colin with surprise. 'What do you mean?'

'Fancy coming to a bar with me? Or we could go have a proper meal somewhere? These canapés are amazing, but I could eat ten times what I've already eaten and still be hungry.'

'Colin, that's very nice of you...'

'I can sense a *but* coming after that.' He smiled at her. 'Can I add a *but* of my own?'

'Of course.' Erin could feel herself blushing.

'Okay, *but* if you do change your mind and ever fancy having a date with a lawyer two floors down, promise me you'll get in touch.'

'I will,' Erin said warmly, still pink. She drained her glass, only her second for the evening. She was still all hot and bothered as Colin gave her a little half salute, then headed away to join everyone else who hunting around for bags and jackets.

Raffaele's cocktail parties were always lavish and always brief. He opened his house in a show of generosity but there was always the unspoken understanding that no one outstay their welcome.

Erin watched the gradual exodus of people but remained where she was, standing by the bay window with the empty glass in her hand.

Her boss's house was magnificent, an exquisite, vast Georgian mansion in one of the best postcodes in London, with grand Corinthian columns and ironwork balconies as intricate as lace. The floor-to-ceiling windows that they guarded were impressive from the outside and even more impressive inside because of the light they let in.

They had all been ushered through to the largest sitting room in the house, whose marble floors with handmade inlays oozed opulence. Lots of pale colours everywhere and an abundance of paintings, all vaguely recognisable and all priceless originals.

Erin had only ever been into a couple of rooms on the ground floor but she imagined that the rest of the magnificent house was the same—cold, elegant and luxurious. Not her thing, if she was honest. She thought of where she had grown up and stifled a smile. *Definitely* not her thing.

She blinked her thoughts away and found that Raffaele was seeing out the last of the fast-departing crowd. Then he turned, lounged indolently against the wall and looked at her with raised eyebrows.

The man was stupidly beautiful.

Six foot two inches of pure, sexy alpha male. His Italian heritage was evident in his classically beautiful features, in the dark hair which he wore slightly too long and in his Mediterranean colouring. Only his eyes, a deep navy blue, suggested other roots. Those eyes were fixed on her now in a lingering, amused stare.

He began strolling towards her.

'Why are you still here?' was the first thing he asked when he was towering over her. 'Shouldn't you have been at the front of the queue when everyone started leaving? You're usually the first to go. Plus…is that an empty glass I see you holding?' He looked at it with an unduly shocked expression.

'I'm not teetotal, Raffaele. Why wouldn't I be holding an empty glass?'

'You didn't drink at the last do I had. I noticed.'

'You *noticed*?'

'It's my job to notice what my employees are getting up to. You didn't touch a drop—although, in fairness, you had a cold and spent most of the evening trying not to cough. I notice things like that. It's why I'm so successful and such an amazing boss.'

'That's very modest of you.'

'You still haven't answered my question. Why are you the last to leave? No, before you answer, let's get out of here. Let's have a drink in the blue room. I want to talk to you about something interesting that came up in one of my discussions with Archer.'

Typically, he didn't give Erin time to answer. He spun around on his heels and headed to the door, grabbing a bottle of champagne on his way 'I'm taking it that you're not in your usual rush to leave?'

'I can stay for another drink.'

Raffaele grinned approvingly and Erin was cross with herself for reddening.

He got to her. She hated to admit that, even to herself, but the man got to her. Even though she never, ever showed it. She was utterly professional in her dealings with him, fully aware that anything else would be as good as signing a death warrant on her very, very well paid and very, very satisfying job.

The blue room was one of the smaller sitting rooms that led into an expansive conservatory and out to the back lawns which, by London standards, were ridiculously big.

'So,' Raffaele said, the second they reached the blue room, 'what's going on with you and the lawyer? Was that why you were hitting the bottle?'

He nodded to one of the sofas. Erin obligingly sat down and waited for him to join her—much as she didn't particularly want to have him so close to her right now. She was fine sitting next to him, arm brushing arm, if they were poring over a report or looking at something on his computer, but in this setting…

Instead, though, he topped up their champagne

glasses, then strolled over to the gleaming console by the window. He perched against it and looked at her with keen interest.

'I beg your pardon?' Erin said.

'You and the lawyer. Something else I noticed. You can tell all, although I have to warn you that I'm not a fan of intra-office affairs...'

'What are you *talking about*, Raffaele?'

'Colin. Grey suit...neat hair...good brain, I admit, but looks like his social life might revolve around dogs and long country walks in bad weather...'

'There's nothing going on between myself and Colin. And, by the way, that's not a very nice description of him! He happens to be a lovely guy! Also,' she spluttered furiously, 'it would be none of your business anyway if Colin and I were dating!'

'You both work for me.'

'There would be no conflict of interest! And I don't even know why we're talking about this because...because...' Erin gulped down a mouthful of champagne and then waved one hand in a dismissive, annoyed gesture.

'Okay! It was simply an observation. I wouldn't want my invaluable secretary to start hearing wedding bells and thinking babies.'

'I don't believe I'm hearing this. And not that it's at all relevant, but I'm not the sort of woman who goes on one date with a man, hears wedding bells, thinks babies and immediately decides to hand in her resignation!'

'Thought not,' Raffaele said smugly. He sipped the champagne and walked towards her, sitting down and relaxing back on the sofa next to his PA.

She looked, he thought, a little ruffled but he was pretty sure that she was telling the truth. Not that it really was any of his business if there was anything going on between her and Colin. Co-workers were free to date one another. It was hardly as though Erin could clamber onto Colin's shoulders to get a promotion or to be given any special treatment. The clambering on shoulders would have to be for a different reason entirely, he thought, slanting a wicked, sideways glance at her.

Still, he felt quietly satisfied that they *weren't* dating, or about to start dating. Was he possessive when it came to his prim and very proper secretary? Only, he decided, insofar as he didn't want to lose her to any heady romantic nonsense. Who else could fill her shoes?

He looked at her for a few seconds through lowered lashes. He could understand Colin's interest in her. Underneath the neatly groomed exterior, Erin Fisher was a lot sexier than first impressions seemed to suggest. Something about those calm, greeny hazel eyes, the silkiness of her poker-straight shoulder-length chestnut hair, the slightly cool expression, the surprisingly husky voice…and the fact that she did nothing to promote herself.

She could be as sensual as any woman a thousand times more overt.

He shifted and cleared his throat.

'So onto the Archer business. Seems like there might be a prospect of another takeover in the offing although this one would be completely out of my comfort zone. Wouldn't mind hearing your thoughts on it but nothing leaves this room. Understood?'

'Before we get onto work, Raffaele, and I do wonder

if we should stick to talking about another acquisition on Monday in the office…'

'Those walls have ears. And, like I said, this is just something I'm toying with…'

'Right. But I stayed behind because there's something I wanted to talk to you about.'

Erin noted the way Raffaele stiffened, the way his eyes narrowed. 'I'm not sure I like the tone of your voice. Tell me you're not handing in your resignation.'

'Why would I be handing in my resignation? What makes you say that?'

'It's not like you to pull me aside to have a word.'

Erin took a deep breath. Was she so predictable that deviating from business talk was something that might set off warning bells in his head? Yes, she was, because she was the employee with no personal life. She was one-dimensional. Maybe that was why he'd been so disconcerted to see Colin flirting with her.

'I happen to be very happy in my job,' she told him firmly.

'If it's a pay rise you're after…'

'I'm not after a pay rise and maybe you could just let me finish?' She'd brought her small cross-body bag in with her and now she dived in, retrieved her phone, unlocked it and handed it over. The screen displayed the relevant thread of texts, the same messages that had been making her phone beep at her throughout the cocktail party. All from Raffaele's ex-girlfriend.

'Ah.'

'"Ah"?' Erin parroted. 'Is "ah" all you have to say, Raffaele? "Tell Raffa I adore him… Could you arrange a meeting…? I know I could get him back if I get the chance…"' She took the phone and stuck it back in her bag. 'Is "ah" your only response to all those texts that have been pinging every five minutes while I've been here?'

Her lips thinned and she drew back and folded her arms.

'You're doing your head-teacher look.'

'This isn't a joke, Raffaele. I resent the fact that your ex-girlfriend thinks it's okay to text me about your relationship!'

'We don't have a relationship.'

'I know that,' Erin said, torn between unbridled resentful sarcasm and a modicum of restraint because he was, after all, her boss. 'I know that because you get me to do the dirty work for you *all the time.*'

'Sorry? I'm not following you.'

'Raffaele, how is it that I always seem to know when you change girlfriends?' She met his perplexed frown with a look of frustrated impatience. 'I know because at the end of every fling, you get me to send them some kind of overblown parting gift.'

'Ah, yes. Occasionally I admit I've asked you to buy them something…'

'"Occasionally" is an understatement.'

'Well,' he said thoughtfully, 'you're a woman. Wouldn't you instinctively know what another woman might like when a relationship comes to an end?'

'*That,*' Erin snapped as temper overrode restraint, 'is possibly the most sexist thing I've *ever* heard you say.' She saw his lips twitch and realised that he was gently poking fun at her, which only made her angrier. 'Buying parting gifts for all those women who enter and exit your life through a never-ending revolving door was never in my job description!'

'"Never-ending revolving door"? I had no idea you had such strong views on the matter, Erin.'

'Well, I have.' Jumping in and out of relationships wasn't Erin's own style. She had been brought up to respect the sanctity of love. Her parents might have had their unusual ways, might have had a taste for moving around and for adventure that was a little too highly developed given they were parents, but they adored one another and they adored her. In their own, eccentric way.

'But that's not even the point. All this…these texts from Alexa. Raffaele, it's an invasion of my privacy.'

'Why would she have decided to text you? Have any of my exes texted you in the past? Tried to get in touch? You've never mentioned a word of it to me. If you were unhappy about the situation, then you should have said something, Erin. You don't find me that unapproachable, do you?'

Erin realised that she had drained her glass of champagne and that he was pouring her another, his expression solicitous and concerned.

Was she overreacting? She cast him a jaundiced look and accepted the glass, gathering herself to get to the point she was determined to make. That any involvement in his fast-paced, superficial love life was beyond the bounds of her employment and that the endless string of texts tonight had only brought that home to her.

Was she now supposed to play ad hoc therapist to all those women he picked up and then dispatched the minute he got bored with them?

She had met Alexa a couple of times. A very nice girl with an excellent clothes-horse, legs-up-to-armpits figure and a posh cut-glass accent. She had been to the office a handful of times and Erin had always winced at the unconcealed adoration in her big, blue eyes every time she looked at Raffaele, knowing what must be coming all too soon.

Honestly, Erin had often thought, *he really doesn't deserve it.*

She'd said nothing, of course. But now she was determined to lay down a few laws. Better late than never.

'I don't find you unapproachable,' she said coolly, 'which is why I'm now taking this opportunity to tell you that you need to find someone else to do the present buying for you. I'll continue to arrange the theatre and the opera and wherever else you want to take those poor girls you date, but buying them farewell gifts to ease your guilty conscience isn't something I want to carry on doing.'

She saw the shutters instantly slam down on those hooded deep blue eyes. His expression cooled and Erin flinched, not only because she thought that she might have crossed a line but because…

Because this was an area into which their relationship never strayed and she didn't like it. She was accustomed to his careless teasing, the warmth of his charm. Not this remote expression in his eyes as he looked at her unsmilingly. This was an expression he had always reserved for other people, people who didn't live up to his exacting standards. Never her.

'I apologise for…overstepping the mark, Raffaele.

I suppose those texts from Alexa were the final straw and also…'

'Also?'

'Nothing,' Erin said quickly as her thoughts turned to her parents again and this time anxiety nudged past the rose-tinted memories.

'In that case, let's go ahead and establish a few boundaries right now. No more favours.' He held up both hands in a light-hearted gesture but his blue eyes were steely. 'I won't be asking you to buy any flowers or jewellery or whatever else I've asked in the past. I will instruct any woman I date to refrain from making personal calls to my office. If anyone gets through, feel free to cut her off without explanation and you can simply tell me that there's been a call. Likewise, there's no need for you to make small talk if one of them happens to inadvertently stray into my office. That way, none of them will be encouraged to think that they have any kind of personal relationship with you. You can be what you're paid to be in situations like that…namely, my very efficient gatekeeper.'

'Raffaele, that's not what I've been saying. Because I… I mentioned that—'

'Let me finish,' he interrupted coolly, 'on another note and while we're setting down boundary lines, you should refrain from making personal observations about my life choices when it comes to women. They're not "those poor girls"…'

'I didn't mean—'

'Oh, but I think you did, Erin. Don't think I haven't glimpsed a certain expression on your face when you haven't seen me looking, an expression of disdain. Why do you think that the women I date are poor girls?'

'Perhaps I used the wrong phraseology.'

'They're anything but poor girls. In fact, I'm a one-woman man and when I date a woman, she has one hundred percent of my focused attention. She has whatever she wants, money no object. You know that well enough because of the things you've booked, which I now discover you booked with simmering resentment.'

Erin could only look at him miserably, hating the horrible vibe between them, desperately wishing they could return to their familiar footing.

But things had to be said. She told herself this and swept aside her discomfort.

'Okay,' she agreed. 'You won't hear another word from me about what I think about your love life.'

'I don't use any of the women I date, Erin. It's not a revolving door, as you put it, of tormented, discarded exes weeping into their hankies and thinking that their lives are over.'

'I never said that!'

'I'm not interested in commitment and I tell that to every single woman I date from the outset. I make it crystal clear that while I'll enjoy them, *enjoy us*, for a while, it's never going to last. Alexa was upset when we broke up but she knew from the outset that it wasn't going to lead to a walk down the aisle, so guilty conscience? You couldn't be further from the truth. Block her from communicating with you and I'll contact her and repeat what I patiently told her four months ago when we started dating.'

'Two and a half months ago.'

'Come again?'

'Nothing,' Erin said quickly. His eyes were still flint hard. She loathed it. She took a deep breath and went for it.

'I probably wouldn't have mentioned anything about the texting, Raffaele, but…' Erin hesitated because this would be the first time she'd ever said anything really personal to him and it felt as though she might be jumping off the edge of a precipice. Yes, she might tell him vaguely what she did on the weekend, share one or two details about a holiday she might have had, but that was where the sharing ended.

'But…?'

'I've been a little stressed lately.' She lowered her eyes and felt her heart begin to thump. 'It's…it's my dad…'

'What about your dad?' Raffaele looked at Erin's downturned head, the glossy hair dropping in a heavy curtain to her shoulders. This was the first real awkwardness to ever crop up between them, which was amazing considering the length of time they'd been working alongside one another.

He knew that he could be a tough taskmaster but not once had he ever thought that she didn't keep pace with him.

She'd opened a can of worms by telling him what she thought about his private life. Naturally he had had no choice but to pull up the drawbridge. He was as transparent as a pane of glass when it came to the world knowing what woman was on his arm, but judgement on how he conducted his private affairs? Out of bounds.

He certainly wouldn't be lectured on commitment. It wasn't on the table. Never. Not for him. From nowhere, he thought of his parents, a marriage that was a sham, a pretence that made him realise a long time ago that behind what passed for love between two people was often a very different reality underneath. And into that cold union, a child with wants and needs could get lost and forgotten.

He slammed shut the door on those uncomfortable thoughts. Erin could make her own decisions, but for him, safety lay in relationships that promised nothing.

Still, it was inexcusable that she have to contend with the fallout from a relationship gone wrong. He was also shocked at how much it cut to the core to have had this stupid spat with her.

He didn't like to see that wounded look in the eyes of someone who was always so calm and cool and composed and efficient. He didn't like to see the slump of her narrow shoulders.

She was about to confide in him and maybe, he mused with a spike of interest that he instinctively knew had always been there, the sound of a door slightly opening between them was a good thing…

It was bizarre that he didn't have any insight at all into her personal life. He wasn't asking for a ring side view of what she did and thought but a few details might not be a bad thing…

His curiosity ratcheted up a few more notches.

He could sense her hesitation. Didn't she realise, he thought wonderingly, that the more she hid the more he wanted to probe?

Especially now that she had offered him this once-in-a-lifetime opportunity?

'Is he okay? Your dad?'

* * *

There was genuine concern in Raffaele's voice and that alone was sufficient to make Erin relax into the conclusion that she had done the right thing. It was ridiculous to act as though she had to fight to the death to protect every square inch of her privacy. She wasn't a secret service spy facing a firing squad if she didn't!

'He's had a fall and broken bones in his ankle. He's going to be off his feet for a bit…'

'Well, that's not too bad, is it? I thought maybe there might be some serious illness involved. You've never mentioned your father to me…or your mother, for that matter. I'm presuming that you have both your parents?'

'I have,' Erin replied briskly. Her eyebrows shot up. 'Come to think of it, *you* haven't mentioned your parents to me either.'

'Valid point.' He flushed. 'You can take a few days off, Erin, if you want to go see them. Where do they live?'

'On the coast.'

'Now if that isn't a broad-spectrum kind of reply,' he drawled. 'Surely you can be a little more forthcoming? I don't intend to drive to wherever they live and pay them a surprise visit if that's what you're scared of.'

Erin shot him a grudging smile. 'Sussex. It's very pretty. I've actually been going there for the past couple of weekends to help out. This is the first weekend I haven't been.'

'I didn't know! You should have said something. You could have made them into long weekends without using up whatever holiday allowance you have.'

'I… Yes, thank you, but there's only so much I can

do at the moment and I've put…well, certain things in place that will help him out until he's back on his feet.'

'Is your father at work? What sort of help did you have to put in place? Surely his company is taking care of everything necessary? Giving him time off and making sure he continues to be paid, arranging whatever physio he needs to have. If they're not, tell me immediately and I can put that right.'

'No, no.' Erin felt a film of perspiration break out. She thought of her parents and their nomadic lifestyle. Until she was twelve, they had lived in a commune not a million miles away from where they now were. It had been a settled and happy time for her, surrounded by families who had all supported one another.

After that, a serious dose of wanderlust had finally got the better of her parents and they had headed out to explore the big, bad world. They had done pretty much every corner of the country, including a stint in the icy wastes of Scotland, and had, only a handful of years ago, arrived in their trusty camper van back where they'd started but in a different part of Sussex.

Thanks to her, they now owned a tiny little house and a small freeholding where they grew their own vegetables, selling the surplus to the local shop. Planning for the future had never been one of their priorities and it had become crashingly obvious that life in a camper van wasn't feasible as a retirement option.

She felt a little faint at the thought of describing her parents' hippy lifestyle to her elegant, sophisticated, sexy boss. She fidgeted with the collar of her shirt, tugging at it, suddenly hot and bothered.

'You don't have to talk about this if it's going to give

you a panic attack,' Raffaele said, vaulting upright and hunting down the bottle. He poured the remnants into their glasses.

'Of course I'm not having a panic attack! I… I'm just saying that I've been a little stressed out about my dad and… Look, it's no big deal, Raffaele, but he doesn't actually have a job. As such.'

'What does "as such" mean?'

'He… My parents live a simple life…'

'I'm really not following you.'

'They own a small freeholding and they're self-sufficient. They grow all their own food, or try to. My mum makes jewellery and has a side job upcycling furniture. I… With my dad's ankle out of action, he hasn't been able to get to do the crops and there's only so much Mum can do so I've been a little stressed out but I've got someone along to help out until my dad is back on his feet…'

Raffaele digested this in silence for a few seconds, unreasonably shocked by the picture she had painted.

Self-sufficient? Selling jewellery? Upcycling furniture? He couldn't have imagined a different background. Actually, he'd pictured accountant married to schoolteacher. Now that she had opened up about a more colourful childhood, he was downright intrigued.

However, he could see that she was already half regretting letting him have that fleeting glimpse of Erin Fisher the woman, as opposed to Erin Fisher his dependable secretary, always kitted out in neatly tailored clothes, always wearing sensible shoes and always sticking to the straight and narrow.

He thought about her flirting with Colin and realised that he didn't like it. Maybe that was why he'd been so relieved when she'd shot his speculations down in flames.

Or had that been a case of the lady protesting too much? Was there something going on there, a furtive romance kept under wraps because they both worked for him? He was irked at the thought of the other man knowing more about his enigmatic PA than he did.

'Sounds like a great life,' he said non-committally as he stood up, waiting for her to follow suit. He was definitely going to dig deeper now. He lowered his gaze so that she couldn't see just how curious he was in the woman who now seemed so much more fleshed out after only a few remarks, a few revelations that most women would never have considered keeping to themselves.

'Maybe.'

'At any rate, keep me in the loop and I'll be at hand to help if you need anything at all.' He smiled lazily at her as she faffed around sticking her bag over her shoulder and adjusting it, her silky chestnut hair swinging across her delicate face. 'And can I say something now that we've been a little more open with one another?'

'What?'

She looked at him warily and he could tell that she had already retreated back behind the facade he was accustomed to.

But they were in new terrain now and just as he felt when he made a new deal, he was filled with the excitement of a challenge. The challenge of getting to know his PA better. Why not? It could only make their harmonious working relationship even better because it would be a more rounded relationship.

'You think I play the field and leave a string of broken hearts behind me,' he murmured, stepping towards her and fleetingly wondering what it would feel like to sift his fingers through that silky hair.

'I never said...'

'Well, I think you should live a little. From the sounds of it, your parents have lived quite the adventure...so how is it that you haven't? Or maybe you have and I've just never seen that side of you...' He tilted his head to one side and wasn't surprised when there was no answer forthcoming.

Was even less surprised at the realisation that seeing those other sides to her was something he really rather wanted to do...

CHAPTER TWO

ERIN HAD NO idea what to expect when she pushed open the door to her large, airy office on the Monday morning at eight sharp, half an hour before most of the workforce began making an appearance but usually a couple hours after her workaholic boss had been at his desk.

Her office was linked to Raffaele's via a bank of sleek walnut sliding doors with panes of smoked glass. If he happened to be in a meeting and needing privacy, the doors would be shut but mostly when he was in, they remained open so that she could, with a glance, see whether he was busy or not.

If her office was large, his was five times the size, large enough to incorporate a separate seating area and a scaled-down boardroom. Many an evening had been spent there working to wrap up a deal.

Right now, as she divested herself of her cardigan, she was relieved to see that the doors were shut.

It gave her more time to continue going down rabbit holes berating herself for confiding in him, when she'd spent so long avoiding that particular trap.

Amid all her heated thoughts as she'd tossed and turned in bed the evening before, the one that jumped out at her was the one she was least willing to confront.

Feelings for her boss, which she had only ever entertained now and again before stuffing them away and pretending that they didn't exist, could no longer be ignored because they went a long way to explaining why she was so rigid about maintaining her privacy with him.

Yes, she disapproved of his antics when it came to the opposite sex. She scorned the way he picked women up, enjoyed them for a while and then discarded them before moving on to the next one. And of course she knew that however attractive the man was for her on a personal level, he could never prove a serious temptation because she could never emotionally engage with a commitment-phobe.

She wanted that love her parents shared. She wanted the guy who would lie down on the railway tracks for her. She might be realistic when it came to her parents' life choices, living on the road and kidding themselves that tomorrows were never going to get in the way of their enjoyment of the present, but on the emotional front…? They had set a template for her to follow and it was firmly embedded in her.

She'd had one stumble, a stumble that was in the past, a stumble, she liked to think, that had been a valuable learning curve. A broken heart had stiffened her resolve never to fall for the wrong guy again, to look carefully at the man she would one day trust with her heart.

Raffaele, with his casual disregard for permanence, represented everything she found unappealing.

So that being the case, why should she have such strong opinions on what he did or didn't do? On any of the choices her boss made? Shouldn't she be indifferent to whatever chaos ensued from his unregulated private life? So what if he asked her to buy presents for the women he always ended up walking away from? It was hardly a back-breaking chore. In fact, it often allowed her an afternoon off, scouting through stupidly expensive stores she would never otherwise have entered, and that was sometimes very entertaining. So why the ruffled feathers?

And why should it matter what her boss knew about her background? She was aware that it was an unorthodox one but she wasn't ashamed of her parents. Yet the thought of him teasing out the details of her personal life made her feel vulnerable, made her feel as though she was advertising herself as a woman rather than as an automaton created solely to play the role of Personal Assistant.

Her rebellious eyes were fond of straying in his direction and only she knew her darkest fantasies, so deeply buried that they were only allowed out at night, when her mind was allowed to wander.

They were forbidden and delicious but they were *contained.*

Was there a disturbing jealousy swirling around inside her at the thought of him and the catwalk models he was so fond of?

She eyed the closed door, took a deep breath and then briskly walked towards it, gave a perfunctory knock and slid it open.

Raffaele was sitting behind his desk, which was as big as a single bed. He was sprawled in the leather swivel chair, his long legs extended, his eyes closed and his hands folded behind his head.

The minute Erin walked in, he opened one eye, then both, then sat up, pulling the chair towards the desk and looking at her with his head to the side.

'You haven't brought my coffee,' he said provocatively. 'I'm very thirsty.'

'The doors were shut. I thought you might have been in a meeting.'

'Only with my thoughts.'

'I didn't realise,' Erin said politely, 'that having a meeting with your thoughts necessitated closed doors.'

'Anything to improve the thinking process. How was the rest of your weekend, Erin? How's your father doing?'

Erin was instantly disabused of the hopeful notion that he might have forgotten what she had told him.

'Good. Thank you.'

'Which bit? The weekend or your father?'

'Both. Shall I fetch you some coffee, Raffaele? There are a few things I wanted to ask you about the Saudi investment fund. I had a look at it, as you asked, on Friday and—'

'Coffee first, Erin. My mind isn't on hedge funds at the moment.' He shot her a smile without taking his eyes off her face.

'Now that we've entered this new and exciting phase in our working relationship, I think it's vital we keep the connection going. I've always thought that it's important that co-workers have more than just a superficial relationship. A three-dimensional relationship really expands our ability to work productively together.'

'Really? I don't remember you mentioning anything of the sort in all the time I've worked here.'

'Haven't I?' He frowned with an expression of puzzlement. 'Perhaps,' he continued as his expression cleared, 'that's because you've always encouraged me to keep my distance and naturally I would never have disrespected your boundaries by being curious about you in any way, shape or form…'

'I'm not the sort of person who spends a lot of time trading confidences,' Erin said impatiently.

'Which I'm sure is something we'll get to in due course.'

'I don't think so,' Erin countered as politely as she could.

Raffaele grinned, stood up and took his time stretching. 'Been here since six,' he said. 'Stiff joints from sitting in a chair for too long.'

Erin didn't say anything. She thought that his joints might have been a little less stiff if he'd made *himself* a cup of coffee but actually she welcomed the opportunity to regroup in private. Of all the things she had expected, a direct reminder of what she'd told him hadn't featured.

Why she would expect subtlety from her outspoken boss she had no idea, but as she scuttled out of his office, half sliding the doors shut behind her, her head was in a whirl.

She'd been comfortable watching him from the sidelines. She had been very happy having her harmless fantasies, safe in the knowledge that theirs was exclusively a working relationship. And if, in the deep recesses of her mind, she saw the possibility of something more, then there was no sign of such wild abandon in her dealings with him.

Having moved from pillar to post during her formative years, sometimes attending school for months on end, sometimes home-schooled by her parents or else just burying her head in books and doing the learning herself, Erin had become a private person.

It had been difficult to make friendships when she wasn't around long enough for them to flourish and although she had had a couple of boyfriends, one reasonably serious when she'd been at university, she had always found it difficult to open up, to show the softer, more vulnerable side of herself.

She knew that that was why the guy she'd dated for over a year had broken up with her. He'd wanted more of *her* than she'd known how to give. He'd wanted someone, he had thrown at her, 'less inhibited, less uptight'.

'You're a nice girl,' he'd said from halfway out of the door, shaking his head in frustration, 'but I don't know who you really are, Erin Fisher, and no one ever will unless you learn to open up! You're bloody hopeless! What man is ever going to be interested in a woman who can never let her hair down! Complete waste!'

How his parting shots had stung, had made her feel incomplete and helpless. Those biting words had made her scared to take more risks on love just in case she made another mistake, another misjudgement. She would take her time and not be rushed into having her choices dictated by her biological clock.

She would only risk loving if certainty of that love being returned was as guaranteed as was humanly possible. She would do her utmost to protect her heart and never let it be damaged again. *Never.*

A crush on her boss, because that was what it was, was perfect because it had allowed her to press Pause on doing anything proactive about her love life.

Abruptly finding herself on the receiving end of his curiosity was a lot less perfect, especially as she only had herself to blame.

Erin made the coffee. Suddenly, after years of pleasant hibernation from dipping her toes in the dating game, she wondered how she had ended up where she had.

She was nearly twenty-nine!

She'd vaguely known that at some point in time she would find the guy she wanted to settle down with, but she'd been in no particular hurry to get there.

Maybe, she thought ruefully as she headed back to the lion's den, there was more of her parents in her than she'd thought.

She'd always considered herself so responsible. She'd stuck to the straight and narrow like glue, unlike her forever wandering parents, who had never really paid attention to how their thirst to roam the world had affected their only child.

Yet when it came to finding a soulmate, it seemed as though she was as meandering as them. The one guy she'd hoped might be the soulmate her heart sought had turned out to be a disaster and so she had hidden away behind a silly secret crush.

How did that begin to make sense? There was a life out there waiting to be lived. She thought of Colin asking her out and wondered now whether she should have taken him up on his offer.

'Just what the doctor ordered,' Raffaele said as soon as she returned to his office with the two mugs of coffee.

Erin didn't say anything but she felt a surge of anger that all this tortured self-analysis had been instigated by her boss and the way he was encroaching on her private terrain.

'You're not completely helpless, Raffaele,' she said a little more acidly than she'd intended. 'You know how to make a cup of coffee for yourself. You don't need to wait until I come.'

'Bravo. I like it!' Raffaele came over and took a mug from her hands, but didn't draw away, a wicked glint in his eyes. As always, he towered over her.

'What? What do you like?' Up close like this, Erin could see the deep blue of his eyes as he stared at her with satisfaction. She could smell the vaguely woody scent of whatever cologne he was wearing. Her heart picked up speed as she stared, doing her best not to flinch away from the directness of his gaze.

'I like hearing you really exercise your voice.'

'I have no idea what you're talking about.'

'You're standing up for yourself!'

'I didn't think I was ever *not* standing up for myself, Raffaele. I've always told you what I thought when I haven't agreed with something you've said…or done.'

'Ah,' he returned, 'but only when it came to work. And naturally, whilst I've appreciated everything you've had to say, it's heart-warming to hear you find your voice when you challenge me on a more personal level.' He nodded to the chair in front of his desk, and Erin obediently sat down.

'You told me that I wasn't allowed to have opinions on your private life, Raffaele. Or have you forgotten that you said that?'

'That's in a different category,' he said smoothly. He still hadn't sat or moved away, so that Erin had to crane her neck to stare up at him. 'What I'm talking about here is you being authentic when you rebut something you don't like. Of course, this doesn't mean that you're excused from making my coffee. On a practical level, you're a much better coffee maker than I am.'

He finally moved to sit back down in his swivel chair and Erin felt her breath return and her pulse normalise.

So he welcomed *her voice.*

Well, she thought, this might actually work for her. If she felt free to answer back to him, then surely it would break the spell he seemed to exert over her? Was he right? Was a more easy-going, well-rounded relationship between them something that was desirable? Had she put Raffaele—or his attractiveness, at least—on some sort of pedestal and fed into that unhealthy addiction by shying away from him? Like some kind of adolescent unrequited crush?

Something easy, something safe she could retreat behind because, after her break-up all those years ago, she was scared of risking her heart with another man? Scared and, unlike so many girls her age, not petrified of entering her thirties without a guy by her side and so in no rush to fix the situation by actually going on dates?

'So,' Raffaele continued, looking at her over the rim of his cup as he sipped the freshly brewed coffee. 'No, no, no…don't get out the laptop just yet. Didn't I just tell you that I'm not having a hedge fund moment? And don't look so alarmed. I haven't suddenly taken leave of my senses.'

The dark, semi-sexy, lazy charm flowed around her and she was more conscious of it than she usually was because they weren't relating to one another in the usual way.

She stared at the space just over his shoulder but it was still far too easy to take in the white shirt, cuffs rolled up to the elbows, the strong, bronzed forearms, the dark hair curling around the strap of his dull matte silver watch strap, the sharp contours of his beautiful aristocratic face.

For a second she thought of her own appearance, regular features, her straight chestnut-brown hair, green eyes, slender and neat and serious. If he was an eagle, she was a sparrow.

'I had no idea there were times when you weren't thinking about hedge funds or investments or company takeovers or exciting mergers.' Erin liked the way this sudden openness between them felt because it gave her a chance to be sarcastic, to gently take him down a notch or two.

'I hope you're not too disappointed.'

'I'm surprised,' she said honestly. 'You're such a workaholic.'

'But I'm not really, am I? You of all people should know that, considering you've only recently staged a rebellion at buying goodbye gifts for the women I go out with.'

Erin flushed.

'I just want to say at this point,' Raffaele murmured soothingly, 'how glad I am that you finally got it together to tell me how you feel about buying those trinkets for my ex-girlfriends. I admit that sermonizing about my relationships is out of bounds, but buying presents? Definitely good of you to remind me that that's not in your remit.'

'Not exactly *trinkets*, Raffaele.'

Raffaele shrugged. 'They are to me,' he said kindly. 'Or maybe a better way of putting it is… I may not commit to permanent relationships, but when they're over, it's my way of thanking the women for the time they've spent with me and the enjoyment they've brought to my life.'

'That's very noble,' Erin said politely, and Raffaele grinned.

'I've never been called *noble* before but I'm more than happy to run with that. But now, moving on to other things...'

'Yes!'

Back to work, Erin thought with relief. Relating to her boss like this was out of her comfort zone and she was keen to return to where she was more sure-footed. Even if it made sense to build a more three-dimensional relationship with him, this was an early stage and she would need time to get used to the subtle shift in their relationship.

Gradually.

She could feed him small sound bites on a day-to-day basis, always with the proviso that she didn't have to confide any more than she felt was necessary, however much his curiosity might have been piqued.

A Pandora's box hadn't been opened. Far from it.

She felt much better after this bracing internal pep talk. 'Do you want me to prioritise the emails that came in at the end of last week? I know you've scanned them all, but there are quite a few I can handle and dispatch myself. You can sign them off by the time I'm ready to leave this evening.'

Raffaele looked at Erin from under his lashes for a few seconds in thoughtful silence.

She looked exactly the same as she did most days, bar

slight variations in colour schemes. Neat skirt, grey, neat short-sleeved shirt, pink with fine white stripes, neat black flats, hair glossy and tucked behind her ears, secured on either side with tortoiseshell clips, and yet the more he looked, the more intensely pretty she seemed. Those delicate features and the huge hazel eyes that were so good at revealing nothing whatsoever. Or had been, until two days ago. That change had been very satisfying indeed.

Outside it was a balmy summer day but where everyone else her age might have turned up the volume on colour, dusted off the cobwebs and brought out the flowered dresses, Erin was as background as she always strove to be except…

She wasn't really background at all, was she?

Raffaele felt the kick of curiosity about her again, this time a little harder. An internal alarm rang distantly, but it was easy to ignore. He was well practised when it came to self-control. This intense curiosity might jar a little because it was out of the ordinary but when it came to women, he was immune to being thrown off course.

He waved aside her enthusiastically professional response. 'Sure. Of course I'll sign off all those emails and by the way, much appreciation for your diligence on the weekend.'

'Is there something more important that you'd like me to do? Before I finish up what I started working on on Friday?' she asked.

'Now that you mention it…'

'Yes?'

'Remember my little drinks party on Saturday?' It was a provocative introduction to what he wanted to say, and Raffaele was amused at the way she unconsciously stiffened.

Yep, she certainly remembered it and he knew why—it was the first time she'd opened up to him about anything. It had made him realise, with surprise just how work oriented their conversations always were and just how cleverly she had always avoided mentioning anything significant about herself.

Her reticence, he now thought with a certain amount of admiration, was a refreshing change from women who were always keen to tell him anything he wanted to know about themselves.

He decided on the spot that a closed book could be a lot more alluring.

Her cheeks were pink and she'd lowered her eyes and was twiddling her fingers on her lap.

'Remember I mentioned a conversation I had with Archer?' He rescued her from her discomfort and saw her breathe a sigh of relief.

'I can't remember who Archer was, I'm afraid.'

'Tall guy...grey hair and a lot of it...some might call it a mane...much younger wife with enough jewellery to open a store.'

Erin smiled and Raffaele realised how much he liked to see her smile. They were a rare sight, and lit up her face in a way that was infectious.

'She did jangle quite a bit. The upside of which was that you always had fair warning of her approach. Sorry, very catty remark.'

Raffaele laughed and looked at her appreciatively. 'Archer's disposing of one of the arms of his leisure business. He wants to specialise in casinos and he needs to sell his chain of hotels so that he can reinvest the money into expanding the gambling side of his business, both the physical premises and creating more of an online presence. I'm thinking of branching out of the money markets and dabbling in something a little less predictable. I'm getting a tired of dealing with tech and hedge funds.'

'Really?'

Raffaele shrugged.

He thought of where he was and what he had inherited. Enough money at the age of twenty-one to take his first-class degree in Maths, convert it into a Masters in Business and not have to worry about the cost. Enough money to decide where he wanted to set his sights and pursue his end goal, without fear of being thrown into poverty if he failed.

Wealthy parents...substantial trust fund... He had increased that original trust fund a hundred times over since he had come into it. He had devoted his career to what he had known and what had come easily to him. A flair with numbers had set him up to turn straw into gold when it came to the money markets, mergers and acquisitions. There had been no need to be a workaholic but he had nevertheless been compelled to throw himself into work, because work was always going to be more reliable than emotions. Work would never disappoint him the way people continually had. He was, he thought bitterly, the archetypal man with the privileged life whose soul was empty, and no amount of money could fill that void.

He was the guy who had never known the real warmth of parental love even if he had been the recipient of everything that money could buy. He couldn't remember either of his parents ever hugging him. And that was before he'd discovered that his parents' marriage was nothing more than a sham, his father's affairs protected from scrutiny in the name of the status quo and power.

Still, that hadn't been enough to kill off his juvenile illusions about love. He had stupidly thought that still… there might be hope for him. Had idiotically ventured into a relationship that had conclusively shattered what little remained of his rose-tinted view of the world.

Disconcerted by this sudden plunge into introspection, Raffaele frowned and dismissed the past with the ease born of habit.

'I can afford to get bored and try my hand at something else,' he said smoothly.

'You're so spoiled,' Erin told him drily. 'I hope you never say anything like that in the public forum, Raffaele, because that's a sure-fire way to lose friends and *not* influence people.'

'Since when do I care what other people think of me?'

'You care what the women you go out with think or else you wouldn't spend a small fortune buying them trinkets when you break up with them.'

'Don't you mean getting *you* to buy them trinkets when I break up with them?' He grinned. 'Okay, we won't go there. I don't want another sermon from you.' His grin widened when she glared at him. 'Maybe,' he added as an aside, 'I buy them expensive trinkets to acknowledge the Herculean feat of putting up with me.'

Erin raised her eyebrows. For a few seconds as their eyes tangled, she wondered whether she could sense an underlying seriousness beneath his throwaway remark.

He was so cavalier about his relationships, so grounded in the certainty that he didn't want any of them to go anywhere.

Why? He had always lived a gilded life. Shouldn't he have been rushing to get the next bit of the jigsaw puzzle in place? The wife and the kids and the houses here, there and everywhere?

It was a question she would never ask. Even the thought of stampeding through that kind of barrier made her skin prickle.

'You're right. Let's talk about you getting into the hotel business because you're going through a bored patch.' She smiled, easing back into the familiarity between them she was so accustomed to.

'Interesting way of putting it. I'll email you the list of hotels. Not many. Five, to be precise. One in the Caribbean and the rest in Europe. The one in the Caribbean is dragging the other four down because it needs extensive refurbishment. Has promise to more than pay for itself but Archer's not willing to put the money in because of the casino business he wants to expand.'

'But would five hotels be worth the time and effort?' Erin asked dubiously.

'I'd probably get them at a knock-down price. He's keen to sell and wants them to remain as hotels and not be converted into flats or housing. I've promised to maintain their integrity. I gather the hotels were his first foray into big business and he's sentimental about them. Written into the contract would be a clause allowing him and his wife to continue to stay at any one of them free of charge. He doesn't think there are many potential buyers who would concede to that.'

'But you would.'

'I can afford to be lenient.' Raffaele shrugged.

'Okay…'

'Why do you sound so unconvinced?' Raffaele said with a touch of irritation.

Erin paused. Perhaps he had a point. 'I'm not sure,' she confessed truthfully. 'I suppose… I suppose I always associated you with the business of making money and a lot of it, so five hotels, one of which needs a lot of work, doesn't seem to fit the pattern. Also all the stuff you do is wrapped up in the business world. Either money or tech.' She smiled. 'It would be a challenge, and I *know* you said you want a change and *of course* a change is as good as a rest but even so…'

'It's not all about money,' Raffaele said gruffly. 'Is that what you think? That I'm driven by the desire to make more and more money?'

'I haven't given it much thought.' The conversation seemed to have suddenly drifted into uncertain territory and she couldn't understand why. Surely it had been a harmless enough question?

There was a brief silence and in that silence something fizzed, a tiny electric current zapping between them like quicksilver. It made Erin shiver with a mixture of apprehension, wariness and low-level excitement.

'But—' her mouth was suddenly dry and her thoughts felt muddled and sluggish '—it doesn't matter.' She laughed shortly, breath hitching in her throat because he was still looking at her, his navy blue eyes unrevealing. 'It's certainly not my business what motivates you. I think hotels would be a great thing to get into. I mean… the world's getting smaller and smaller, and people are getting more and more adventurous and the cost of travel is getting more and more competitive. Er…have you had any ideas on what you would do to change the dynamic of what already exists?'

'Small steps.' Raffaele waved a hand although his eyes remained firmly glued to her face. 'Early stages.'

'I could set up whatever meetings you want,' Erin suggested.

'Already had a more lengthy chat with Archer yesterday. He's definitely on board. Of course, the money may not be of a make-or-break figure but that doesn't mean that I'm going to go into something like this without any due diligence whatsoever.'

'No…'

'Which brings me to the interesting part of this deal.'

'Yes?'

'I think step one will be seeing what I'm letting myself in for and the best place to start will be with the hotel that needs the most work.'

He switched attention to his computer and after a couple of seconds he swivelled the screen so that it was facing Erin. She leaned towards it and focused on the online brochure in front of her.

She scrolled past a picture of a tired hotel in a spectacular setting, amid lush rainforests. She flicked through to images of faded plantation-style elegance and then speed-read some of the copy, all touristy bumph.

'So here's where I tell you to make sure your passport's up to date.'

Erin looked at him blankly as her brain registered the question.

'Sorry?'

'Because—' he sat back and spread his arms wide in an all-encompassing gesture '—the sooner we go and see what the deal is with hotel number one, the sooner I can start putting things in place. I've never been involved in the leisure industry. It should prove to be an interesting gamble.'

'We?'

'You'll be coming with me,' Raffaele said comfortably.

Erin's eyes widened with sudden alarm and her heart picked up pace. 'That's not going to be possible, I'm afraid.'

She'd gone on a couple of business trips with him in the past. Short, intense breaks in Paris, Lisbon and Milan, where they had worked solidly alongside the usual consortium of lawyers and accountants. She'd never thought twice about accompanying him but that was before…

Before things had changed between them...

Those subtle changes had shifted the dynamics. It felt ridiculous that telling her boss a tiny bit about herself had altered their relationship so much, but it had. She couldn't quite put her finger on why, because nothing she had said had been very important and yet…

'Why not?' Raffaele asked bluntly. 'Is it because of your father? I know you've been going down to help out for the past few weekends but if your presence is going to be missed so much, then I'm happy to get someone in to do whatever needs to be done outside…harvest whatever needs harvesting. What needs harvesting anyway? You never specified.'

'No!' Erin was even more appalled at the thought

of further inroads being made into her private life. 'I mean—'

'So if it's not concern for your father, then why the hesitation? Do you have any inconvenient pets that might need sitting? That can always be arranged. Kennels exist, to the best of my knowledge. You don't have a dog, do you? Or a cat? Why don't I know this about you? Seems a small detail. Birds? Tropical fish?'

'Raffaele, no pets! No dogs, cats, fish or birds!'

'So where's the problem?' He let the silence settle between them for a few seconds. 'We'll be gone for a week and you'll be richly compensated for the inconvenience, just as you always have been on the few trips abroad you've done with me. So, Erin, all you have to do is sort out the flights and book us a couple of rooms at the hotel. Honestly? I have no idea why you're so alarmed.' He tilted his head to one side and stared at her. 'It won't be any different than any other business trip except this time, we're going somewhere hot.'

CHAPTER THREE

EIGHT DAYS LATER, Erin found herself staring, with trepidation, at the suitcase sitting by the front door of her little rented two-up, two-down terraced house on the outskirts of London.

Fortunately, considering the fact that she would shortly be flying to the Caribbean with him, the discomfort she had briefly felt in Raffaele's presence ever since the cocktail party had faded as they once more settled into the usual routine of work, work, work.

No more curious questions about her private life. No more provocative remarks that made her feel hot and bothered and on edge.

Raffaele had returned to the grindstone and indeed, she hadn't seen him at all for the past four days. He'd disappeared to New York on business.

Yesterday, he had emailed her to tell her that he would send his driver to collect her and take her to the airport. Normally, she managed all his travel arrangements but he knew her well. She suspected that he'd worked out that presenting her with a fait accompli would do away with her predictable protests that she would be more than happy to arrange her own transport, which was what she'd done on every other occasion when they'd travelled anywhere together on business. Fine when it was a short hop at a civilised time during the day. Less fine for a transatlantic long-haul trip at an ungodly hour in the morning.

'I'll be waiting for you in the first-class lounge,' he'd instructed her. 'We can take some time to discuss the nitty-gritty of the hotel accounts and expenditures so that we're prepared for the meetings we'll be having with the hotel manager and his lot and Erin—' even as she'd read the closing sentence of his email, she'd had no trouble picturing the amused grin on his face '—don't forget it's going to be boiling hot and humid over there. Feel free to jettison the woolly tights and starchy skirts.'

Right now, at a little after six in the morning, she was dressed in a loose pair of cargo pants and a short-sleeved T-shirt. She'd thrown the grey cardigan she usually wore to the office over the T-shirt in a nod to the fact that this wasn't going to be a holiday. It was going to be about work and meetings.

She would have felt more comfortable in her usual uniform of a skirt, a blouse and her black pumps, but even she had to acknowledge that that look wouldn't do in searing tropical heat. Not unless she wanted to pass out with heat stroke.

Her case contained an assortment of similarly summer clothes, most of which hadn't seen the light of day since last year when she'd had a two-week holiday in Cyprus with two girlfriends.

She was hovering in her small sitting room, glancing anxiously at her watch, when the doorbell rang half an hour before she was expecting it to. Overtaken by a sudden flurry of nerves, she leapt to her feet and headed for the front door.

She glanced at her reflection in the mirror in the tiny, narrow hallway. She looked young and fresh-faced and not much like Raffaele Rossi's PA heading off for a week of high-level meetings and writing up reports. With one hand on her case and her bag slung over her shoulder, she pulled open the door—and drew in a sharp breath, her eyes widening in shock.

'Raffaele!'

Her boss stood on her doorstep lounging against the door frame, hand raised as though on the verge of ringing the doorbell again. He was casually dressed in black jeans, a black polo shirt and uberexpensive tan handmade loafers. The absence of all logos proclaimed just how pricey his clothes were.

'What are you doing here?' Erin asked.

'I thought it might be fairly obvious. I've come to collect you to take you to the airport.'

'I was expecting George!'

'Sadly George had to pull out at the last minute. His wife's been rushed to hospital with a burst appendix. I thought it might be a little insensitive to tell him to drive us to Gatwick first before going to the hospital to hold her hand. Open up and let me in. I have time for a quick coffee before we head off.'

'That's awful!'

'What's awful? George's sudden health crisis with his wife—' Raffaele grinned '—or my unexpected appearance on your doorstep?'

'George, of course!'

'I'll be sure to pass on your condolences.'

'I could have taken public transport,' Erin huffed as she continued to guard the door with folded arms.

'I wouldn't dream of letting you take public transport to the airport, Erin. How would you get to Gatwick from here, anyway? I don't recall passing any Tubes on the way. Or maybe I passed one a thousand miles back.'

He nudged the front door and Erin reluctantly stepped aside.

Raffaele had never been to her house. There had never been any reason for him to have visited. Now that he was here, she could feel a tide of mortification rising up inside her.

So there *wasn't* a Tube. There was a mainline station which she took to Waterloo and then it was easy enough to connect with whatever Tube she wanted. Granted the mainline station was a hearty walk away but there was no such thing as too much exercise.

The area was respectable enough and the house was acceptable enough, and her landlady was a dream who had allowed her to paint the walls and hang one or two pictures and plant whatever she'd wanted to plant in the back garden.

But as she looked at her boss turning a full circle in the small hallway, she mentally cringed because she knew that this wouldn't have been what he would have expected, not given the amount he paid her.

'I can make you a coffee if you like,' she offered, breaking the telling silence briskly, 'but perhaps it might be a good idea to get to the airport early? We'll be less rushed if we discuss business once we're there.' She remained where she was, arms folded.

* * *

Raffaele focused his eyes on her for a few silent seconds.

Frankly, he was shocked.

Why was she living here? In a faceless, nondescript suburb miles from public transport, never mind cafés, restaurants, shops and any sort of buzzy infrastructure suitable for a girl of her age? The nearest he had found to any sort of life had been a strip of uninspiring shops on what passed for the high street. Several had been boarded up.

She was paid a small fortune!

Where was the money going? How many more layers were there to peel away to reveal the real Erin Fisher? How was it that in *four years* he had succeeded in finding out less about her than he'd found out about the guy who delivered his post?

Curiosity tore through him but he nodded slowly and agreed.

'Good idea. You can fill me in roughly on any background information you've got on the hotel group. General stuff. We can hit the details later when I've got my computer in front of me and I'm not behind the wheel of a car. Where's your bag?'

'It's okay, I can carry it.' Erin grabbed her compact suitcase, which she'd left by the front door, glanced around her one last time.

As he passed by her through the front door, Raffaele could see her mind working—making sure she hadn't forgotten anything, mentally double-checking that everything that should be turned off was turned off and everything that should be turned on was turned on. Everything he never had to consider when he left on trips; he had others to worry about those things for him.

Finally, Erin stepped out and locked up.

'Sure you have enough in that small case?'

'It's not a holiday. It's a work week, so I've taken pretty much what I would wear for a work week.'

'But excluding,' Raffaele murmured, sliding an amused sideways glance at her, 'the starchy skirts and blouses...'

Erin huffed her way into the passenger seat of Raffaele's sleek, black Ferrari and didn't respond to the jibe.

'Well?'

He turned to her when he was in the car, flicking on the engine but staring at her for a few seconds as he waited for her to answer.

'No starchy skirts. Raffaele, you made that clear in your email. I've googled the weather over there so obviously I haven't packed my tights and fleecy jumpers and overcoat.'

Raffaele burst out laughing and pulled away from the kerb.

'What about swimsuits?'

'What about them?'

'Any tucked away in your very small case?'

'I had no idea I would be needing those for a working holiday,' Erin said tartly. 'Are we planning on conducting meetings in the ocean?'

Raffaele was still laughing as she fetched her notebook from her handbag and began prepping him on all the non-essential details of the hotel chain that might not seem immediately relevant but which might hold the key to whether he acquired the properties or not.

This was something Erin was especially good at.

She'd worked hard to get to university and she'd known, the minute she started doing her research, that the best courses would be the ones that led to concrete jobs. She'd studied accounting and finance with a view to becoming a chartered accountant but along the way had got spooked at the promise of a job that would require very long hours doing things that seemed too repetitive to be satisfying, at least for her.

Plus, her parents had been entering an unstable time of their lives, ready to settle down but without the money to buy anywhere at all. They were getting older, with their mobile home looking like it might be their forever home, so she wanted a job that paid well but didn't consume her every waking moment. She needed to be there for them when they inevitably needed her.

When they'd been younger, they'd managed just fine but now that they were no longer moving around, Erin could see how much they had aged over the years.

They'd had her very late in life and now were both in their late sixties and bewildered by modern life, which seemed to have passed them by in their colourful, adventurous travels. Their computer was a thousand years old and only used for the most basic of tasks.

She'd had to introduce them to technology bit by bit and had realised that any job that demanded all of her time wasn't going to work, and besides she wouldn't enjoy it.

She'd had some interesting temp jobs while she waited for just the right one to come along and sure enough, the role as Raffaele's assistant had fallen into her lap and had been sheer perfection. She'd been able to use everything she'd learned at university and had enjoyed delving into the details of projects without having to devote her entire life to them. She'd loved having the challenge of new things happening week after week whilst also maintaining a switch-off mode so that none of those new challenges became onerous.

She rattled off her findings as he drove, satnav guiding them on the fastest route. Raffaele listened with his head tilted to one side, interrupting to ask questions, nodding in agreement with some of her conclusions and then congratulating her on a thorough job when she'd finished.

'My perfect little PA,' he eventually murmured with satisfaction, 'what would I do without you?'

'I'm guessing you wouldn't curl up in a corner, sobbing and crying and thinking that the sky had fallen in. You'd just find someone else.' Erin glanced across at him with a wry smile and then kept looking, first at his aristocratic profile, the crooked smile on his mouth and then at the capable, long fingers holding the steering wheel. She had to tear her eyes away.

'Took me a while to find *you.* Do you remember what I told you about the long line of failed applicants?'

'You mean the ones who just couldn't help falling in love with you?'

'Inappropriate crushes, I believe is what I said.'

'Maybe you just made them a little nervous, Raffaele. Or maybe if you'd widened the pool to include a few candidates over the age of thirty, you might have had a little more luck.'

The scenery was whizzing past them. She lived closer

to Gatwick than Raffaele did and they were well on their way now, speeding towards the airport and with next to no traffic on the roads because it was still early.

'You weren't over the age of thirty and I don't make *you* nervous,' he pointed out. 'You settled in to my routine like a duck to water from day one. No blushing every time I looked at you…no stammering if I asked a question… no showing up in inappropriate outfits…'

'Sorry, but I thought you were quite critical of my dress code.' Erin settled back against the plush leather seat and half closed her eyes.

It was a stupid car. Who needed something this fast in London? But she had to admit that it was comfortable. Raffaele had once told her that he didn't get to drive as often as he liked, so she could understand why he hadn't delegated the task to someone else even though after New York he surely would have been a tiny bit jet-lagged.

People stared, mouths open, as the black Ferrari rushed past their more pedestrian cars on the motorway.

It was ridiculous to be tickled pink by that but Erin was.

'Your dress code is perfectly acceptable. Although I've questioned it when you've shown up at Christmas parties in pretty much the same outfits as you wear to work.'

'I don't have wardrobes filled with cocktail dresses.'

Raffaele slanted a sideways glance at her.

Erin's delicate, pale face was drawn. He took in the outfit, her interpretation of 'casual'. Workmanlike cargo trousers, a T-shirt and a cardigan which she'd wrapped around herself.

He was only now realising just how little she put herself out to impress him on the physical front and just how surprising that was. Nearly every woman Raffaele had ever met had always done their best to impress him. Given the chance to show up in casual gear, Erin had chosen the least feminine outfit she could have got her hands on, even though the loose, unfussy clothes suited her slender frame, made her look incredibly feminine.

With a small jolt, he realised that being in her presence soothed him somehow. When he considered his life, the relationships he'd had… First, there was his cold, distant upbringing, carrying with it those hard lessons of hurt, sadness, disillusionment and eventually the erection of icy walls behind which his heart would forever be locked. Then that one crazy fling with a woman all those years ago who confirmed his belief that romantic happiness was beyond his grasp. It had been a painful reminder of his own inability to love; he'd tried but he just hadn't had enough to give. After that, he had walked away from anything that required too much emotion of him. And now there were the women to whom he gave trinkets when everything ended. Fun, energetic, temporary.

Between all that, Erin occupied a special place.

She stimulated him intellectually and without a physical connection…yes, she soothed him, made him feel safe.

And now, more than that…she intrigued him.

What had she meant when she'd said that she didn't have wardrobes full of cocktail dresses?

Did she hate cocktail dresses?

Because on her pay grade, she could certainly buy as many as she wanted. That thought brought him back to her house. What was going on there?

He dumped pointless introspection about his past and focused on the here and now. The suddenly very invigorating here and now with his once-predictable secretary. She had her secrets and he'd find out all about them in due course. It was a very pleasant prospect.

They were going to have a week together and not all of it was going to involve sitting in front of a computer or having back-to-back meetings with hotel people.

Next to him, Erin yawned.

'You're tired,' he said.

'I got up really early,' Erin agreed. 'Plus I went to bed really late. I wanted to finish doing as thorough a job as I could on researching the hotels and it took me a bit longer than I thought. I never knew the hotel business could have so many nooks and crannies. It's not straightforward at all. The profit and loss columns are, but then things can change at the turn of the dice. If the restaurant in one of the hotels gets a new chef and the menu isn't popular, business could fall off and that could affect the profit margins in a matter of weeks. If something happens that spooks the clientele, same could happen...'

'Something like what? Murder in the building?' Raffaele grinned but he was still half thinking about her living circumstances and tempted to ask her what was going on there.

'You'd be surprised. I started checking out all the things that could go wrong in hotels, impacting their profits, and there's a lot.'

Erin shifted so that she was half turned to look at him.

'I still don't get it, you know,' she murmured drowsily, on the edge of nodding off in the sleek, powerful car.

'Don't get what?'

'Why you're interested in buying this chain of hotels. It feels like a real departure for you. And feel free to tell me to mind my own business but I'm just looking at it from a practical point of view. I know you said that it's not about the money but I always figured that, with any luck, people end up doing the things they really enjoy and are good at and then they stick to the programme and don't really deviate. And you've always seemed to thrive on the challenges of the financial world.'

'A change is as good as a rest, as you said. Is that what you did? Never deviate? Were you never tempted by any other career choice?'

'I…' Erin blinked. She seemed to think for a second. 'No. Financial security is important to me,' she said firmly. 'I also didn't think that we were talking about me.'

'Now that we're getting to know one another a little better, I think that conversations between us should be fluid, don't you? Airport up ahead. We made excellent time.'

The conversation was lost in a whirlwind of valet parking and checking in and then, within half an hour, they were in the first-class lounge, ushered through the opulent, semi-empty space like royalty to a group of comfy chairs and brought coffee and breakfast by one of the uniformed staff who was clearly in awe of Raffaele.

And then they carried on chatting about work.

Her comfort zone, Raffaele mused. He looked at her from under his lashes as she busied herself on her laptop, swivelling it occasionally to corroborate whatever point she was making. He intended to dig much deeper into his guarded secretary than she might anticipate.

Why the sudden fascination? Had it always been there, lurking under the surface, waiting for the right key to unlock it?

Or maybe he was bored of his standard-issue women. Bored with ridiculously good-looking women who were always too eager to please. Maybe he needed the safe distraction of someone like Erin, someone clever and restrained and, even more important, someone who wasn't in awe of him, who would never want any sort of romantic involvement with him. Why shouldn't he give in to curiosity about his disciplined, guarded secretary with all those enticing layers?

One day he would settle down, although right now the thought alone was enough to bring him out in a cold sweat. Too many associations with his parents and their dysfunctional marriage, two people wandering around their mansions, barely connecting on any meaningful level. Too many memories of his youthful hopes shot down in flames because the girl he'd thought he'd loved just couldn't put up with a guy who had no heart to give. He thought of all the many ways love could fail and his mind went blank.

Why was the past resurfacing right now and with such vigour? Raffaele didn't know, but it made no difference. He was firmly rooted in the way he was. He would never change.

He was here, Erin was here and she had challenged him by revealing just a little bit more about herself than she ever had before. He'd never been one to resist a challenge so right now, Erin was irresistible.

'Are you listening to what I'm saying, Raffaele?'

Raffaele smiled slowly at her. 'I'm always listening to what you say.'

Erin reddened. For a couple of seconds, she appeared to be lost for words. She stared down at her computer; Raffaele watched, lazy and amused and interested.

'Good,' she told him huskily when she finally dragged her gaze back to him, 'because I've done a lot of work on these hotels…and a lot of background research into the hospitality trade.'

'I'm getting the picture. Definitely beyond the call of duty. No need for you to have stayed up working into the early hours of the morning to collate all this material. I may be a hard taskmaster but even I have limits. You told me you were curious about my sudden interest in branching out from the well-trodden path.'

Someone came around to tell them that they could board and Raffaele stood up and waited for her to follow suit.

'I'll tell you why…' He picked up where he had left off and fell into step alongside her, looking down at the smooth, silky, chestnut-brown hair that swung in a shiny curtain on either side of her face. The little clips restraining it were somehow prissy and sexy at the same time. 'I came into a sizeable trust fund when I was twenty-one, enough for me to play around and take my time discovering what I was really good at. It was a privilege. I had the luxury of only needing brains and drive to get where I wanted to go. A very gifted guy I met a few months ago, Alessandro Barbieri, had equal amounts of brains and drive but he also had obstacles to deal with that I never had. My trust fund was brilliant but there's no such thing as a free gift, at least not in my corner of the world with my wealthy parents.'

'How so?' Erin looked sideways at him with wide, curious eyes and shivered as his deep blue gaze lingered on her face.

'Part of the condition of my trust fund was to continue working for the family company as a form of long-term repayment of the money being granted to me at such a young age. Had I chosen to take my trust fund later, when I was in my early thirties, it would have come with no strings attached. My parents could have waived that condition but they chose not to.'

'So there was no rush for you. You could have gone to work for your family company, knowing that you would come into a lump sum when it was time for you to settle down and get married.' She smiled. 'You're an only child. Maybe they couldn't bear the thought of an empty nest.'

Raffaele's lips thinned. She couldn't have been further from the truth. His father had always enjoyed power over other people and that had included him. For Franco Rossi, love was control and control could be cruel.

Somehow he had got lost in his explanation but now he found that he was enjoying the rare experience of opening up to someone else. This wasn't weakness. He had casually mentioned something that could be found anywhere on the internet if you could be bothered to sift through all the bumph about him that had been posted over the years.

The details of his background were all there for anyone to see. Erin knew that he was an only child and he couldn't remember ever having mentioned that to her. It was just general knowledge.

If he had elaborated on the bare bones, then it just came under the heading of chit-chat with a woman he actually spent the majority of his life with.

'Empty nest? No. You haven't quite got that right.' His voice was bitter and as their eyes briefly met he noted her startled look. He forced a tight smile. 'I actually paid back every penny of the trust fund as soon as I was financially able to so that I could sever any hold my parents might have felt they had on me. Then I worked furiously to replenish my resources. But now that I have more than I could ever possibly need, I fancy doing something I was never geared to do but was always interested in pursuing.'

Walking at pace and not looking at him, Erin felt a slow flush of heat within her. This sharing of confidences felt incredibly intimate.

She wondered whether Raffaele was aware of the change in his tone of voice, the disillusionment that had seeped through at that passing mention of his parents.

'That's brilliant,' she said warmly but she didn't glance across at him because she realised that she didn't want this moment to be over quite yet. It was like having a taste of forbidden fruit—exciting, irresistible… dangerous.

She'd always had a lot of insight into his work ethic, into his many and varied relationships with the opposite sex…into his utter lack of commitment on that front, but she had never had any inkling of his buried dreams or unfulfilled desires, had never once heard him mention his family.

Was that what she was now glimpsing? *The real Raffaele that no one ever saw?*

Or was she letting her imagination get the better of her?

Was this stuff he routinely told other people but had never told her because she was his employee? She always suspected that Raffaele only revealed what he wanted to reveal, that he was, at heart, an intensely private man. But maybe he was, in actual fact, the sort who spilled his heart out to every one of those women he hopped into bed with.

Maybe there was nothing he loved more than a bit of post-coital breast beating and emotion sharing.

No.

Her gut told her that the things he'd just told her were feelings he'd probably never shared with anyone and the heat spread through her again.

'I admit I love what I do and I've always been invested in the importance of having financial security...' Thoughts of her parents and their casual disregard for anything that smacked of putting down roots or planning for a future sprang to her mind. 'But I've always been interested in painting...'

'Painting?'

'No need to sound so shocked, Raffaele,' Erin laughed. She'd barely noticed that they'd been checked through and were now heading to board the plane.

She'd travelled first-class with him before on business trips and every time she'd been impressed all over again by the sheer luxury. The plush bedding, the flat bed, the gourmet à la carte dining and the all the little extras as well, none of which she had ever taken advantage of.

Now, though, as they were shown to their seats, which were side by side and as comfortable as armchairs, Erin barely noticed the opulence around her or the fawning of the good-looking crew eager to hand them flutes of champagne.

As she settled in and half turned to look at him, she felt the thrill of danger zip through her again.

Tomorrow she would *definitely* put all this wild curiosity to rest but in the meantime…

Her eyes drifted treacherously to Raffaele's forearm resting on the wide leather armrest between them. Bronzed, muscled, strong.

She looked away guiltily.

'I've always absolutely loved drawing but with all the travelling we did…'

'Travelling? What travelling? I always got the impression that the Greek islands and Rhodes was the extent of your travels.'

'I meant…' Too late, Erin realised that she was on the verge of sharing way too much.

What was going on here, she thought with a flare of panic? Had she forgotten that Raffaele was *her boss*? She had worked hard to make sure that boundaries between them were always maintained. She had known from day one that he didn't tolerate inappropriate behaviour from the women who worked for him. That had suited her fine because she was, by nature, guarded and self-contained.

So what was happening here?

Did she really want to jeopardise her job for the sake of satisfying her curiosity?

Worse, was she beginning to think that because she had shared a little more of herself with Raffaele and because he had said a couple of things about *himself*, that they were somehow striking forth on some kind of relationship? That they were now going to be sharing little confidences and eyeing one another across their laptop computers?

Had she *taken leave of her senses*?

She thought about the crush she'd had on him for *years*. Had that managed to scramble her brains?

She strapped herself in and reached into her bag for the book she had brought with her, a pointed reminder to herself that she wasn't here to make incessant small talk and tell him all the ins and outs of her private life.

The thought of having to face him in an office setting after a series of indiscreet confessions filled her with dread.

'I meant that I've always *wanted* to do a lot of travelling, landscape painting. It's an impractical dream but yes, I suppose if I could have, I might have chosen to study fine art but…' She shot him a wary look and began opening her book to her bookmarked page. 'Not many of us have a trust fund to be going on with.' She smiled at him, one of her practised cool, unrevealing smiles. 'Do you want to carry on working on the flight over? I know it's going to be a long one. Or is it okay if I read my book?'

She turned her focus to the page, even knowing that Raffaele was still staring at her. Only when he tilted the book, forcing her to look up, did she meet his amused gaze.

'What are you reading?'

Their eyes tangled and he grinned. 'Looks verbose.'

'How can you tell anything from the cover?' Erin tugged the book and he released it but carried on looking at her.

'I can't. I'm going on the blurb at the back. I can't say that "a moving and epic poetic masterpiece" is the sort of thing I would find captivating.'

'It's riveting. Can I ask what does interest you?'

'Nothing poetic or epic. Feel free to devour your book on the flight over. I have a lot of work to attend to so you can settle down in comfort without fear of being interrupted. You'll probably fall asleep on the flight over.'

'I don't think so.'

'Even with a bed? You can also change into pyjamas. There's a luxury pair waiting for you so that you can really relax.'

'I'll stick to my book.'

'Of course you will but I'd be shocked if it doesn't put you to sleep.'

He was still grinning as he flipped open his laptop and she settled into the enormous seat and made herself comfortable.

Fall asleep?

Pyjamas?

She'd rather drink twenty cups of black coffee and prop her eyelids open with matchsticks.

She stared at her book while her mind chattered away, diving off in a million different directions.

The next sound she heard was the captain's voice congratulating himself on an excellent and turbulence-free flight.

She was nudged into consciousness and blinked her way to the surface to see Raffaele's face way too close to hers for comfort. There was a cushion under her head and, horror of horrors, she was propped up on his shoulder.

'Ah, Sleeping Beauty's awake!'

'You should never have let me fall asleep!'

'And deprive myself of the chance to hear you snoring? Wouldn't have dreamed of it. But it's wakey-wakey time now. Our adventure's waiting just around the corner!'

CHAPTER FOUR

WITH THE TIME DIFFERENCE, dusk was already gathering pace as she and Raffaele cleared customs at the tiny airport on the island.

A handful of hours on a plane had transported them from the pleasant warmth of an English early-summer day to blistering tropical heat.

Around them, people were coming and going and talking and calling out to one another. Taxi drivers were hunting down customers, but without any real sense of urgency, taking refusals good-naturedly. There were fragrant smells of food in the air and over the road, Erin could make out a bustling strip of shops selling souvenirs and food.

She stared around her.

It was wondrous—he smells, the heat and the indigo, purple and orange sky blazing above them as night fell.

'Now aren't you glad that you listened to what I said and didn't decide to wear your suit?'

'I've never worn a suit in my entire life, Raffaele.'

But she was too absorbed in this alien, spectacular environment to rustle up much of a response to what he'd said.

'A jacket…a blouse…a skirt… That's as good as a suit. The hotel's arranged a driver for us while we're here.'

The words had barely left his mouth when a smiling man approached them with a clipboard and then they were being ushered through the milling crowd away from the airport towards a car park.

In the distance, she could see the sea, black and still. The heat was like being in a sauna, and it made her slow down.

She felt Raffaele's hand on her back as he gently but firmly propelled her along and she cast one last backwards glance over her shoulder, taking in everything, wishing she could have stayed a bit longer just breathing in the swirl of new, different smells.

She'd travelled so much with her parents. She'd seen every corner of England. For six memorable months of lazy home-schooling, they had explored northern France against a backdrop of incredible spring and summer weather. There had been lots of barbecues on their portable camping stove, weaving in and out of small villages in their caravan, enjoying the scenery and a culture which was different from their home and yet very much the same.

She'd never, ever been anywhere like *this* and every adventurous cell in her body which she hadn't even known existed was fired up with excitement.

They slid into a small, black four-wheel-drive jeep and then they were off, windows down so that a warm breeze blew through.

The hotel was tucked away in the lush rainforest in the opposite direction of the main drag of tourist hotels and motels. She'd glanced at the blurb about it on the internet and knew that it was divided into a handful of little cabins and then the main hotel for guests who didn't like the thought of being too cut off.

Erin couldn't get enough of the scenery passing them by even though, as darkness settled fast, the canopy of towering trees and the dense foliage by the side of the road was reduced to shadows and mysterious dark shapes that harboured the vibrant sounds of tree frogs and crickets and the last of the daytime birdsong.

'This is amazing.' She turned to Raffaele, who was leaning against the passenger door and looking at her. In the darkness, she could only make out the angles of his face and the glitter of his eyes.

The road was bumpy, narrowing in places, widening in others and swinging around corners that were barely discernible in the darkness. She had to hang on to the door handle to steady herself from falling against him.

Ahead, their driver was concentrating on the twisty road to the exclusion of everything else.

'Never been to the Caribbean?'

'No. A bit of Europe and… No, I've never been anywhere like this at all in my life before. Have you? No, strike that. Silly question.' The breeze was blowing her hair across her face. She held it back with one hand and looked at him. 'I bet this part of the world is like a second home to you.'

'Not quite,' Raffaele said drily, 'but I'm not unfamiliar with it.'

The car jolted and she half fell against him, then quickly pulled back as he reached out to steady her.

'I don't know how I'm going to be able to focus on work while I'm here,' she confessed breathlessly.

Something about the fragrant air, the salty smell of distant sea and the unfamiliarity of their surroundings was filling her with a heady sense of adventure that she knew she had to bank down. She distantly recalled the feeling from way back, when she and her parents would be on the road to some new, unexplored destination—a time before she'd woken up to the reality that no amount of adventure could ever be worth the insecurity of never knowing what lay around the corner or the loneliness of an adolescence in which friends were always just passing through.

She thought she'd ruthlessly killed any streak in her that might have been tempted to follow in her parents' footsteps, but it was obvious that in her soul a bit of their influence lingered. She could feel it now.

'You won't be on call 24/7,' Raffaele murmured. 'And remember what I said about *living a little*?'

In the semi-darkness, the deep blue eyes resting on her were lazy and speculative and Erin felt her pulse begin to race.

'I can do that in my own time.' She cleared her throat. 'Not on company time.' She winced at just how prissy she sounded. Like a middle-aged woman instead of a girl in her late twenties. 'By which I mean,' she rushed into embarrassed clarification, 'of course I'm going to take time out to enjoy myself while I'm here. I know it's not going to be around-the-clock meetings and there'll be a lot to explore.'

'I'll make sure you have a driver to take you on tours.'

'Really?'

'The public transport infrastructure here is basic, Erin, and I'm pointing that out now, before you tell me that you can manage perfectly on your own just so long as you can locate the nearest Tube.'

'Very funny, Raffaele.' But his throwaway remark suddenly stung. He was just teasing her. She knew that. It wasn't out of the ordinary and normally she would have swatted his teasing away without really noticing it at all. But for some reason, out there with the smell of excitement in the air, it seemed to compound the sudden image she had of herself as stuffy and inhibited and dull. The person her ex-boyfriend had been considerate enough to describe in great detail.

'Who knows? I might even come with you on some of your out-of-hour tours. Might be useful to gauge the infrastructure, if I'm to take over Archer's hotel business.'

'I thought you were familiar with this part of the world.' She thought of them touring the island together without the benefit of a laptop acting as chaperone and her stomach lurched.

'I'd be looking at it from a slightly different standpoint,' Raffaele drawled. 'On the few occasions I've been to this part of the world, it hasn't been in the capacity of a fact-finding mission.'

'I can imagine.'

'Can you?'

Erin shrugged and turned away to look out of the window once more although she could feel his eyes on her. Eventually, with the silence thickening between them, she returned her reluctant gaze to his face.

'What will be the timings for tomorrow? I know we have a schedule but I'm not sure how much we're going to adhere to it. Do you want me to be up and running at the usual time? Eight? Maybe we could discuss the day's projections before we have the first meeting?'

'I've noticed something about you, Erin.'

'Really?'

'The second you begin feeling a little bit uncomfortable with a conversation, you swiftly steer it back to work. Have you noticed that about yourself?'

'I've noticed that the hotel is up ahead.'

Their eyes met. He smiled slowly and half nodded but she wasn't sure whether he was nodding in agreement or nodding because she'd just proved his point.

He looked at the approaching bank of lights and Erin could sense the change in him as his business mind took over. Even from a distance, he was already assessing the venture he might eventually be sinking money into.

The bumpy road wound its way towards the hotel. Through the rustling trees on either side, Erin could see various paths leading out into the forest to the individual cabins she had read about.

Lanterns lit up the veranda of the main building and people were sitting outside, eating and drinking. Only a handful, fewer than she might have expected.

'Hope you remembered to book cabins, like I asked,' Raffaele turned and said. 'I thought that separate cabins might be more relaxed in terms of work, more convenient for private debriefing. Everything we discuss will be informal, just a matter of useful observations, and then if I decide to go ahead, I can get my legal team involved along with the useful suspects. If you'd rather stay in the hotel, then that's fine. The entire resort caters for approximately fifty guests but from the looks of it, it's not running to full capacity.'

'It's such a shame because the setting is amazing. And yes, I did remember about the cabins and no, I'm happy with the cabin. It makes sense in terms of work to be away from the hustle and bustle, as you say. Not that there seems to be much of the hustle or the bustle.'

Raffaele hmmed. 'The place has potential but I doubt it'll ever make millions. Fortunately, I can afford to take the hit if I decide to go ahead with this. It's late but feel free to head to the restaurant for something to eat or have something delivered to your cabin. I'm going to catch up on work and we can reconvene tomorrow morning eight sharp in the hotel foyer. Sound acceptable?'

'Perfect.'

'The first meeting is with the guy in charge of running the place. We'll meet him at nine thirty and aside from showing us around, he'll give us a general feel for how the hotel is doing financially and what improvements would need to happen to take it forward.'

'Wonderful.'

'And no need for the swimsuit just yet. The meeting won't be ocean based.'

He was still grinning at his own wisecrack, she noticed, as they headed into the hotel to be greeted by staff who fussed over them as they checked in.

It was a charming open space with large windows protected by white shutters and overhead fans that made the heat just about bearable—although now it was much cooler than it had been when they'd arrived.

Through the open windows, the light breeze brought in the rich scent of the tropical flowers and the sounds of an orchestra of night creatures lurking in the encroaching forest outside.

The decor was colourful with a huge painting of tropical birds behind the reception desk, and the wooden planters by the entrance were filled with cascading ferns and lush, vivid flowers that were bigger than anything Erin had ever seen before. Like everything else around her, they seemed exotically, fantastically alien, reminding her of just how little she'd seen of the world, despite her parents' wandering feet.

She glanced across at Raffaele, who was signing the usual check-in forms, asking a few questions about their accommodation, and was struck at the enormous gulf between them.

He'd barely looked around him. He'd seen it all before even if, as he'd said, it hadn't been on 'fact-finding missions'.

She imagined his trips to the Caribbean had been more along the lines of playboy-having-fun-in-the-sun excursions.

All of a sudden her childish crush…those little shivers of awareness…the warmth that had flooded her when he'd thrown her some breadcrumbs of personal information about himself… They all seemed pathetic and embarrassing.

'Right. Ready?'

Erin blinked and focused on the drop-dead-gorgeous guy staring down at her.

'We're all checked in?'

'Certainly are.' Raffaele handed her back her passport and began heading out, waiting for her to follow him. One of the staff members led the way, chatting as he walked ahead of them, telling them about the restaurant, about the availability of car rentals or driver services, about the capital, which was by the sea and excellent for local restaurants and interesting souvenir shops.

They left the main hotel behind. Here, lanterns lit various diverging pathways into the forest and under the canopy of overhanging trees, the sounds of the insects and night animals seemed more insistent.

Erin unconsciously sidled a little closer to Raffaele.

It was now after nine yet the air was still hot and sultry and everywhere smelled of lush, rain-washed foliage. That made sense; it was supposed to be the wet season—although, as the hotel porter leading the way to their accommodation observed, there was no real difference between the wet and dry months. Sometimes rain in December and sun in July. Only the Big Man up there knew what was going on, he said.

'I'll walk you to your cabin,' Raffaele said as soon as their porter retreated back into the darkness of the forest.

Erin hovered, looking around her anxiously.

Her cabin was close to his, separated by a bank of thick bushes which were dark, rustling silhouettes under the semi-moonlit, star-studded sky. The hotel they had left behind a mere handful of minutes ago felt like a million miles away.

'Do you think we're safe here?'

'Come again?'

'Safe.' Erin cleared her throat nervously.

'We both live in London. I'm going to be bold and say that it's probably going to be a lot safer out here on a peaceful island in the middle of a rainforest. Rampant knife crime tends to stick to big cities.' He made a show of looking around him for people carrying knives and Erin could see the glint of his teeth as he tried to control a mix of indulgence and amusement. 'Erin, there's no need to worry. Honestly. I don't hear any suspicious noises. Have you decided what you're going to do about eating? I'm not sure if you heard me ask when I was checking in, but there's room service out here although the hot food stops at nine thirty and after that it's snacks and sandwiches. The place is also well stocked with snacks and drinks.'

They were at the door of her cabin. It was small but perfect, with a small wooden patio at the front. To the side, a hammock was strung between two posts. There was also a similar set-up next to Raffaele's cabin and the clearing was washed under the mellow light of the lanterns strung between the trees.

'I'm not hungry. And I'm not talking about knife crime. I'm talking about creatures,' Erin told him flatly.

'Creatures? What about them?'

'I… There are noises… Can you hear noises? Pretty loud, actually.' She cleared her throat. 'Insects, maybe? Harmless little insects?'

'Ah. I'm getting it.'

'I've never been anywhere like this in my life…'

'You're really scared, aren't you?'

'No!'

He wasn't smiling anymore. The genuine concern in his voice stiffened her spine because, weird noises or no weird noises, her boss wasn't there to hold her hand and calm her nerves.

She fumbled with the old-fashioned key and pushed the door open into a cosy space, easily big enough for two people. She stepped into a sweet sitting room, with a low sofa and a television and small kitchenette. Beyond that, she could see the door that led to the bedroom. Through the open shutters, the breeze gently billowed the thin curtains.

She looked around to see that Raffaele had followed her into the cabin to deposit her bag on the ground and when she switched on the overhead light, his face was gentle.

He walked towards the phone on the rattan console in the small sitting area outside the bedroom and pointed to it.

'Call me if you're spooked by anything, Erin. I mean that. There will also be a phone next to the bed. Believe it or not, there's Wi-Fi here. The password is in the bedroom on the dressing table, according to the guy behind the desk. You can call me anytime on my mobile. I understand that if you've never been to the tropics before, it might seem a little overwhelming. Are you going to be all right?'

'Yes.' Erin folded her arms, mortified at the stupid fuss she'd made. 'Storm in a teacup.'

'Shall I get you assigned a room in the hotel? You might feel more comfortable there.'

'I'll be fine.'

He hesitated, looked at her in silence for a few seconds, then walked towards the door.

Hand on the doorknob, he said with utter seriousness, 'Just as long as you're not too proud to knock on my door whatever the time of day or night if you need me. Understood?'

'I appreciate the offer, Raffaele, but *I'll be fine*. I just need a couple of hours to adjust. The long flight…the heat… It's all been a bit overwhelming…'

That said, within seconds of him shutting the door behind him, Erin set about checking the entire cabin just to make sure there weren't any creepy-crawlies bedding down for the night next to her.

It was a lovely space. Rattan furniture and cute local paintings on the walls and a sofa covered in bright floral patterns. Still, even with her nerves ratcheted up, Erin could detect the signs of wear and tear. The circular rug on the ground was clean but threadbare, the phone Raffaele had indicated earlier was a hundred years old and the small kitchenette looked tired. She was sure that were she to dig a little deeper, she would find far more fundamental issues which would point to failings through the entire hotel. She made sure to firmly shut the connecting door between the sitting area and the bedroom, which was beautifully air-conditioned.

She fell asleep quickly. The flight, the darkness and the array of emotions that had been churning inside her ever since she'd opened her front door to find Raffaele standing on her doorstep had resulted in sheer exhaustion.

She awoke just as quickly and surfaced at speed, momentarily confused and disoriented by unfamiliar sounds. The room was cool but beyond the low hum of the air conditioning Erin was all too aware of the forest pressing against the cabin. The sounds that had been insistent background noise when she'd entered four hours previously had now become a cacophony.

And there was something banging around in the sitting room.

She could *hear* it through the thin wall separating the bedroom from the sitting area.

At first, nerves paralysed her but after a lifetime of frozen fear, she finally managed to leap out of bed, step back into her flip-flops and race into the pitch-black space of the sitting area. When she banged on the light, she caught the swoop of wings racing up towards the high rafters.

She didn't stop to think.

She scooted at lightning speed out of the cabin and only felt safe when she was banging on Raffaele's door.

Raffaele woke fast, muscles reflexively primed before his brain had even come back online.

He didn't run. He walked purposefully to the door and pulled it open. Only then did his brain really engage and, disconcertingly, it engaged in a way he had least expected.

Erin was there. Wearing next to nothing.

Some tiny shorts and a sexy little vest. He could see the rounded shape of her small breasts. Everything that she had managed over the years to conceal under an array of drab clothes was revealed now, from the slenderness of her arms to her smooth, shapely legs and *the tiny span of her waist…*

He felt his breath catch and blood rushed to a place that hadn't been active since he'd broken up with Alexa of the infinite text messages.

Swiftly he moved slightly behind the half-open door because he was only in boxers himself and, *hell*, he had an erection! Rock hard, utterly inexplicable and highly embarrassing. 'Erin…'

'There's something in the cabin!'

'Wait…"something in the cabin"?'

'Raffaele, I'm sorry… I know it's…it's…'

'After three in the morning?'

'I…'

She was close to tears. *His perfect, coolly controlled, unflappable secretary was close to tears!*

Another punch of raw arousal hit him, making him wonder what sort of dinosaur he was if he could be actively turned on by a damsel in distress. Although, in fairness, not just any old damsel in distress.

'Okay. Come in. I'll grab some trousers and don't worry… I'll sort it out.'

He spun around on his heels and disappeared quickly into the adjoining bedroom before his body could betray him even more than it already had.

Erin stepped into his cabin and it was only when he had vanished that two things struck her, temporarily banishing the fear and panic that had gripped her as she'd flown to his cabin.

The first was that Raffaele had answered the door in just his boxers. For the first time her fantasies had crashed slap bang into reality and the body she had idly and guiltily daydreamed about had been there right before her eyes. No amount of daydreaming could come close to the magnificence of the real thing.

Broad, muscled shoulders, sexy dark hair on his chest and a flat belly that tapered to narrow hips.

She'd felt the air leave her body in a whoosh when he'd answered the door and then, before she could really absorb what she was looking at, he'd somehow manoeuvred himself behind the door, probably in an act of kindness to spare her blushes.

She knew he thought she was all those things a brilliant secretary should be—smart, efficient, professional—along with all those things a woman should never be as far as femininity went, *smart*, *efficient*, *professional*, equalled *drab*, *unexciting*, *uptight*…

The second thing that struck her, hard on the heels of her semi-naked boss and his glorious body, was the fact that she had scrambled over to his cabin without bothering to shove on anything over her pyjamas. The sensible dressing gown she had brought with her was still hanging pointlessly on a hook on the bathroom door.

And here she was…

Appalled, she folded her arms, covering as much of her breasts as she could, and waited for him to emerge from the bedroom.

With a sinking feeling, it was dawning on her that whatever had been flapping around in the cabin would have been easier to deal with than this.

'Ready to face the monster in the room?'

Raffaele appeared decently clad in some grey jogging bottoms and a loose T-shirt and flip-flops.

Their eyes met and he smiled reassuringly.

'I shouldn't have rushed over here at this ungodly hour,' Erin said jerkily.

'Why not? Something obviously petrified you and naturally I'm here to help. I can't have you cowering under the blankets until you get rescued by room service in the morning. I'm being serious here, Erin. Want me to carry you back to your cabin? Because I will.'

'Just get rid of whatever's flying around inside the room.' She cleared her throat, eyes darting between his cabin and hers in expectation of just about anything that might lunge out at them. There was a myriad of noises coming from the trees and the bushes all around them. 'Please.'

'Your wish...my command.'

She led the way to her cabin. It was literally seconds away from his. She could feel the blades of grass on the ground brush against her flip-flops and fronds from the ferns tickle her legs. They both heard the sound of furious flapping the second she pushed open the door.

Raffaele didn't give her time to protest. He swept her off her feet, kicked the door shut behind him and carried her straight through to the bedroom.

'Stay here.'

'What are you going to do? What is it making that racket?'

'I'll find out soon enough.'

'Are you scared? Should we call the manager?'

'At this hour in the morning?' Raffaele laughed. 'No and no. By which I mean no manager, and no, I'm not scared.'

He headed out of the room, shutting the door quietly behind him, and Erin curled herself into a ball in the chair by the window and tried her best to block out the muffled sounds outside.

It had been a mistake coming here. She should have made up some excuse and dug her heels in and stayed put in the safety of her office in London. If she had, she wouldn't be here now, trembling at the thought of whatever was out there, not to mention all the other *whatevers* that might be lurking in the bushes and the trees and the rivers, waiting for some unsuspecting English girl with zero experience of the tropics to wander along.

And if she had dug her heels in her boss wouldn't be playing knight in shining armour at her request, and wasn't that the bigger problem?

How had the dynamic between them changed so suddenly? How had one stray confidence turned into…into *this*?

She was only aware of Raffaele's return to the room when he was standing in front of her, casting a long shadow.

She looked up at him with a sigh of resignation, resentful that she was now the damsel in distress.

'What was it?'

He squatted down on his haunches so that they were on eye level.

'It was a fruit bat. Harmless and more scared of you than you were of it. One of the windows was open behind the curtains and it must have got in either accidentally or because it was attracted to the fruit in the bowl on the table. You were really scared, weren't you?'

'I overreacted. I'm sorry. I should never have run over to your cabin and banged on your door.'

'Why not? You were scared and I could help.'

'Raffaele…this isn't me.'

'It is now,' he returned with a crooked smile. 'I like this new Erin Fisher. I like the fact that you can drop the mask now and again. It's definitely an improvement.'

Erin met his eyes. She felt the thrill of her illicit attraction fighting against the *need* for her to return to the person she had been, safe and controlled and in charge of her emotions.

She just couldn't allow a childish crush to overwhelm

common sense. She would never make another mistake with a man again. Finding love didn't lie down that road. She'd made one mistake. *She was wiser now.*

But Raffaele was so close to her. She could smell him, breathe him in, reach out and touch him.

She balled her hands into fists. 'I was temporarily thrown off balance. Like I said, I have no experience of what it's like in this part of the world. Tomorrow, once I begin to find my feet, believe me, I won't be a shaking wreck at the sound of a silly bat flapping around in the living room.'

Brave words. In reality, she honestly wouldn't care whether the bat was popping over to make friends with a cup of tea and some scones; just thinking about it appearing again made her shiver.

'For the record, despite the fact that the hotel is set in a forest, there are remarkably few venomous creatures.' He stood up, flexed his muscles and dragged the chair by the dressing table over to where she was sitting.

Erin watched him warily. If anything, his presence felt more suffocating now, with him leaning into her, forearms resting on his thighs, knees practically touching hers.

'Is that right?' she asked faintly.

'There are snakes but most are harmless. They'll slither away in fear if they hear you coming.'

'What about the less harmless varieties?'

'Don't worry. You won't come across them. We won't be doing any deep-jungle exploring and actually, even if we chose to, I don't think there have been any tales of deadly snake bites on this island in living memory. Anyway,' he said and grinned, 'I'm here.'

'And you have a lot of experience in dealing with venomous snakes?'

'None, but as you can see, I'm good at dealing with the unexpected. The fruit bat won't be bothering you again.'

'No, it won't.' Erin clung to politeness but her heart was thumping as she looked at him, remembering way too clearly how he had looked in his boxers and nothing else, 'because I'll make sure all the windows are shut when I go to bed.'

'Wise precaution.' He stood up, headed to the bedroom door but then he turned to look back at her over his shoulder. 'Now, before you protest, I'm going to settle down in the chair outside and make sure you're okay before I head back to my cabin.'

'Raffaele!'

'Tut, tut, what did I say?' He reached out and before she could pull back, his finger was on her lips in a silencing motion. She felt the blood rush to her face. 'No protests or you might find that I stay for the rest of the morning. Understood?'

Erin didn't protest. She physically couldn't. Her vocal cords had tightened up because all she could imagine was this big, powerful, sexy guy in the room outside keeping watch over her while she slept.

She nodded silently. Even after he'd let himself out of the bedroom, she could still feel where his finger had briefly been on her lips.

But, weirdly, within ten minutes she was fast asleep.

CHAPTER FIVE

In the light of day, Erin's panic the night before seemed like a massive over reaction. She cringed when she thought of the way she'd raced over to Raffaele's cabin like—fittingly—a bat out of hell and flung herself at him, trusting him to deal with the situation with just the sort of helpless, stereotypically feminine reaction she honestly had never had time for.

She could change the washer in a tap, hang a heavy picture and put up shelves! So why had a bit of wing flapping sent her shrieking with terror straight into the arms of her boss? How did this tally with the woman who had privately scorned the many women who'd fallen under his spell and treated him like an Action Man hero every time they were within smelling distance of him?

She also cringed knowing that he had checked on her before he'd left her cabin. She knew he had, because the socks she'd worn to bed just in case she stepped on something in the dark had been slipped off her feet and neatly placed on the chair, and she'd been covered with the cotton blanket which had been folded at the foot of the bed. He had placed it over the thin sheet she had fallen asleep under, knowing that at some point the cold from the air conditioning unit would probably wake her up.

She decided that she would face the day and the upcoming week without dwelling on any of that. It was the only way she would be able to get through their confinement together and work the way she had always worked—professionally and efficiently.

It was a perfect day and jet lag had not yet put in an appearance. At a little after eight, the sky was already a cloudless blue and as she headed out of the cabin, the scenery that had been shrouded in darkness when they'd arrived was spectacular in all its Technicolor glory.

It was hot but the clearing beneath the towering canopy of trees was cool and shady and there was nothing sinister in the gentle rustle of the breeze through the leaves.

The paths they had followed through the forest to their cabins had seemed bewildering when the only light had been from the lanterns strung between the trees but now, in the bright light of a sun filled day, the winding pathways were all visible between the borders of bright tropical flowers and giant, oversized ferns.

She headed straight to Raffaele's cabin and banked down the nerves as she raised her hand.

He opened the door on the first knock.

'Erin.'

'Good morning.' Erin smiled distantly and he grinned.

'It certainly is. Come in, come in. Don't stand there hovering by the door. First meeting isn't until eleven so we have time to brief and grab breakfast.'

He turned on his heels and Erin reluctantly followed him in. He was dressed casually. Navy blue collared T-shirt and a pair of light cream linen trousers and flip-flops.

In her short-sleeved lemon blouse and neat cotton skirt

and with her laptop firmly tucked under her arm, she felt inappropriately stuffy.

'So?' he called over his shoulder. 'Sleep all right for the remainder of the night—or should I say morning? I stayed on for about an hour then went to check on you and you were fast asleep.'

'Thank you for…the babysitting duties,' Erin said politely.

'It was no bother,' Raffaele returned with equal politeness but with a wicked glint in his eyes. 'As babysitting duties go, it was stress free. In fact, all I did was remove the socks and throw a blanket over you.'

Erin gritted her teeth as the very subject she'd hoped to dodge was flung at her with an amused smile and raised eyebrows.

'Won't happen again. I can already see how ridiculous and misplaced my brief panic was. Everything always looks so much less threatening in the daylight. What will we be covering in this morning's meeting? I've brought my laptop so that we can maybe have a look at how the costs of running the place are broken down?'

'Excellent. Let me grab mine and we can go have some breakfast in the restaurant. Unless you'd rather we stay here? Have someone deliver something for us?'

'No! The restaurant will be fine.'

Raffaele smiled and shrugged.

Erin was as formally dressed as it was humanly possible to be given the heat and the humidity. Unassuming flowered skirt, loosely falling to mid-calf, and a neat shirt with tiny buttons. Very impractical, he decided. She would be drenched in sweat within the hour.

He knew just what that was about. She was desperate to put distance between the woman he had seen in the early hours of the morning. The woman half scared to death, wearing the sexiest little vest and shorts imaginable. The woman who had banged on his door looking tousled and pink faced and very, very cute. The woman who had painted toenails—a sweet pale pink that somehow gave the lie to her being the ultimate professional with all girlie traits stamped into oblivion. She was as slender as a ballet dancer and, having seen her in her nightwear, he could now attest that she had the shapeliest legs he'd seen on a woman in a long time.

The woman with the background he'd never have guessed who had roused his curiosity to the point where his curiosity had no intention of being put to bed, at least not just yet.

The restaurant was a charming wooden pavilion attached to the side of the main hotel, open to the birds which flitted in and out, pecking whatever scraps had been left on plates before they were cleared away. Their plumage was bright—blue and yellow and orange—and they filled the air with song.

'This place is amazing,' Erin admitted as they were shown to a table. Around them various other couples were having breakfast and poring over maps and making plans. Shorts and T-shirts with beach bags on the ground. She fidgeted uncomfortably in her more formal gear.

'Yes, it is but there's a lot of work that would have to be done to get it up and running. I was out and about at six thirty and the only real thing it's got going for it is its location, which is stunning. There's a waterfall about twenty minutes' walk away. Beautiful. Very private. These are the sort of things I'll want us to check out because it's the added bonuses that can sell a hotel like this and my feeling is those have been bypassed as Archer's goals have shifted away from his hotel business.'

Erin was busy taking in the birds and the flowers curling on green tendrils over the white wooden railings of the sitting area, where the tables were arranged in no particular order.

She nodded absently and only surfaced when breakfast began appearing.

'Did I order?' She frowned.

'No menu. You get what's freshly baked.'

'That's something else that could be used as a selling point. A lot of people like the idea of the food being locally sourced on a daily basis.'

'So you *were* listening to what I was saying.'

'I always listen to what you say. I'm your secretary. That's what I'm paid to do.'

'Ah…because for a while there you were a million miles away.'

'I was admiring all the birds,' Erin admitted. 'I've never seen anything like it.' She thought of the life she'd led, which she'd always considered eccentric and ridiculously adventurous compared to everyone else she had known along the way, the other pre-teens and the teenagers who had passed in and out of her life like whispers. For a while it *had* been both those things but being here…

It was in places like this, she thought, that the adventure really started. It was here with all the new sights and smells and tastes, where nothing was like anything else that had gone before, that the imagination could take flight.

The predictability of her life at home hit her like a sledgehammer. After her break-up a million years ago, she had retreated into the safety of her carefully curated comfort zone, the very one that had become part and parcel of her life from as far back as she could remember.

She had put *adventure* in a box that wasn't for her and that had included adventures with men.

She'd been moulded by her wandering parents and hurt by her ex-boyfriend, hurt by the things he had casually thrown at her. Protecting herself had become the most important goal in her life.

They were disturbing thoughts and it was easier, surrounded by all this untamed beauty, to shove them aside.

'And this breakfast is delicious. The bread…is there coconut in it?' Their eyes collided and Erin blushed. 'This is what I meant when I said that the food could be a pulling point here.' She cleared her throat and looked away.

'Definitely something I will mention to Gary, the manager, when we meet him later. How did your parents take you being absent from another weekend because you're here with me?'

Erin was thrown by the abrupt change of subject and she blinked like an owl for a couple of seconds.

'Meant to ask at the airport,' Raffaele drawled, sitting back to look at her with his head tilted to the side. 'But we got wrapped up in work chat. How dependent is your father physically on you being there on the weekends? I know you said something about arranging for someone to come and help him…' He paused and looked at her thoughtfully for a couple of seconds. 'Which suddenly makes me wonder something...'

'Shouldn't we stick to working out what we're going to concentrate on when we meet the hotel manager in...' Erin glanced at her phone, which was on the table, and was gutted to see that they still had over an hour before they were due to meet Gary. 'Er...soon?'

'I think our time would be better used having a stroll through the grounds and assessing the property and the outbuildings. Finished here?'

'Yes, sure...'

'Good!' He smiled brightly at her and vaulted upright, waiting for her to follow suit. 'We can start with the cabins,' he said, waiting while she faffed and got her things together.

'My laptop...'

'I'll get someone to stash it in the room we'll be using for our meeting.' He nodded to a member of staff who came along and obligingly whipped it away, leaving Erin feeling vaguely deprived of an essential prop.

'But getting back to what we were talking about a minute ago,' he murmured, slowing his pace so that she could fall in alongside him. 'Can I ask you something?'

'I'd rather you didn't.'

'Really? Why?'

'Because I'd rather we stick to work. Feels like there's a lot to discuss without us getting bogged down in chit-chat about other stuff.'

'Oh, we can spare a few minutes, Erin. Relax and go with the flow for a change.'

'I relax *all the time*, Raffaele.'

'Really? You don't seem very relaxed now. I'm just

making conversation. There's honestly no need to get hot under the collar. This isn't an interview and your job isn't going to be on the line depending on what answers you give me. In fact, you don't have to give me any answers at all. I know we agreed that it would a good idea if we moved our relationship along a notch or two, got it into a more normal place, but if you feel a little panicked at the thought of that, then of course I'll back off and we can return to where we were.'

'Where we were?' This was to buy time, because the ground underneath Erin seemed to have suddenly turned to quicksand. *Why?* 'And I'm not *panicked* at the thought of making conversation with you, Raffaele!'

'I can't tell you how pleased I am to hear that. I feel that we're more than just boss and secretary. I feel that we're *friends*.'

'Friends…' Erin thought of the way her body responded when she was around him, the way her mind soared off into fantasy land with him playing the lead role… *Friend* didn't come close to describing his interaction with her in all her forbidden imaginings.

'So why is it that you had to be the one to arrange help for your father?'

Erin sighed. He was like a dog with a bone. It was one of the many reasons why he was so successful. He was primed to tenaciously pursue what he wanted until he got it. She'd known that; it was just that that tenacity had never been directed at her. But now it was and there seemed to be little she could do about it without giving the impression of being scared, which inevitably would lead him to question why that might be.

Besides, the heat and the sounds of birds and insects,

the smell of the sea in the air, the exuberance of the trees and bushes and flowers all around them…it was all having a lulling effect on her.

Could she bother to be on her guard?

Why should she?

The lesson she should take from all this wasn't that she had to keep her defences up around him just in case he caught a glimpse of her inappropriate crush.

Nor was it that she might shatter into a thousand pieces if she wasn't scrupulous about who she decided to let into her life.

No, what she should take from this was that she needed to get a move on, needed to *start living*.

What Raffaele did or didn't know about her was irrelevant because she wasn't involved with him.

Outside the work arena, he had no impact on her life. She would never tell him how she *felt* about things, what her thoughts were on *love* or *marriage*, and he would never know anything of her dreams or fears or desires.

But questions about her dad?

Not a problem!

Still, that was easier thought than believed…

She idly noted the bees buzzing lazily around giant deep pink trumpet-shaped flowers that seemed to grow wild all around them.

A clutch of cabins was just ahead of them, each private and separated by trees. All had hammocks identical to the ones she and Raffaele had, although these hammocks were knotted, unused because the cabins were empty.

She swatted away some tiny insects from in front of her, realising that she was baking hot in her skirt and blouse.

Bypassing the cabins, they chatted idly about the state of the overlong grass and the signs of decay in the wood, but Erin knew that the topic of her father would reappear. Sure enough, once they'd explored some of the forested area beyond the main hotel and begun to trudge back to the cool of the hotel, Raffaele shoved his hands into the pockets of his lightweight trousers, turned to her and picked up where they had left off.

'I'm too hot to answer any questions,' Erin said irritably, breathing a huge sigh of relief when they were back in the hotel foyer where the overhead fan was generating at least a smattering of cool air.

Raffaele grinned. 'I did think that your outfit might have been a little much for this heat,' he said. 'Did you bring anything lighter?'

'Sort of,' she sighed, sweeping her hair back and feeling it damp with perspiration.

'Sort of? You mean *sort of cotton shorts*? Or *sort of loose clothing*? We'll wrap this meeting up quickly, head into town and get you clothes that will be a little more comfortable while we're here or else you'll find yourself completely overwhelmed by the humidity. In fact—' he glanced at his watch '—you skip the meeting and I'll meet you outside your cabin at twelve fifteen. You can change into something more comfortable. We're not going to discuss anything important anyway so it's not essential you attend. I'll arrange transport into town…'

'Raffaele…'

'No protesting, Erin. The last thing I want or need is a secretary who can't function because she's overcome by the heat.'

'No, I'm sure you don't,' Erin said testily, 'especially

considering you've already rescued me once already. How much more rescuing can you be expected to do before your trusty steed collapses?'

He grinned broadly at that and she glared back, too steaming hot to do much else.

As soon as he headed off into the hotel, she flew to her cabin. She'd packed two pairs of shorts but they weren't decent enough to wear to a meeting. Too old and way too short.

Her skirts, which would have been perfect for an English summer, were ridiculously out of place when it came to coping in a furnace. Buttons on blouses were maddening.

She had a quick shower then changed into another of her stupid skirts and this time one of the old T-shirts and her flip-flops instead of the canvas shoes she had been wearing.

Raffaele knocked promptly on her door at twelve fifteen.

Annoyingly, he looked cool as a cucumber.

'That looks a lot more suitable' was the first thing he said in an approving voice. 'Why didn't you wear that this morning? Don't feel that you have to dress formally while you're here, even if it *is* something of a working holiday. I've got a driver to take us into town. Ready?'

'Guess so.'

'Don't sound so thrilled.' His voice lightened with amusement as he led the way to the jeep that was on standby. 'Don't women love shopping?'

'Not all.'

Once in the back seat of the sturdy little jeep, Erin relaxed back and half closed her eyes.

'All the women I've ever dated have loved shopping. In fact, I'd say that they were all passionate about it, the sort of passion top scientists might feel in pursuit of the cure for cancer.'

'That says more about the women you choose to date than the female species as a whole.' She slanted a sideways glance at him to find him staring at her with a lazy half smile on his face.

So, so unfairly sexy. Her thoughts were sluggish and she didn't look away, not even when he slowly raised his eyebrows in a question.

The car bumped along the very uneven road that had brought them to the compound the day before.

The breeze was lovely and she felt as floppy as a rag doll.

When she finally glanced away from his face, she realised that her hand was on the seat between them as though begging to be held. Honestly, she still felt too lethargic to whip it away. It was as though the intense heat had formed gaping cracks in her usual defence systems.

'Do you financially support your parents, Erin?'

His voice was low and serious and Erin met his eyes without flinching and nodded.

'I was surprised at where you live,' he mused. 'Now it makes sense. You never said.'

'Why do you think I should have said anything?' Erin asked with genuine curiosity.

'Because, like I said, I thought we were friends. Maybe not the confiding-intimate-secrets kind of friends but surely friends who share financial troubles...'

'You would never have any financial troubles to share, Raffaele, and honestly, we're not friends. You're my boss and lines have to be drawn.' She thought of her inappropriate crush which couldn't have been further from the friends category he mistakenly thought they might be in. 'You're used to women who love shopping and who probably can't wait to tell you all about themselves but I'm not any of those women. What's more, I work for you. Don't forget all the girls you had to sack because they started blurring the boundaries.'

'If you'd told me that your father was out of work, then I would have gladly given you whatever money you needed to tide him over until he found something else. Was he made redundant? What did he do for a living?'

Erin looked at Raffaele coolly.

He truly lived in an ivory tower. Born into a life of privilege, handed a healthy trust fund when he was barely out of nappies. Whatever disagreements he might have had with his dad over time, he would never have known inconsistency. He had always been cocooned. From the top of Mount Olympus, it would be impossible not to look down on the ones who lived below without a certain amount of incomprehension and pity.

He would never have had self-doubt and would never have suffered. A squabble over when to repay a trust fund that would set you up for life didn't count.

She thought of how her parents had agonised when they had finally decided to put down roots only to discover how unprepared they were for the reality of what that process entailed.

Her father had cried and apologised to her when she had told them that she would use her own money to ensure their future security. They'd had next to no savings of their own by then. Living in the present had made zero allowances for life in the future.

'You wouldn't understand,' Erin eventually said.

'Try me.'

Erin looked away for a few minutes. It was a slow journey because the roads were narrow, twisty and occasionally perilous, with steep drops into dense forest on either side. She couldn't imagine what would happen if someone happened to be coming in the opposite direction. Strung overhead in a seemingly random fashion, electricity cables bowed under twisting vines. The heat was like a blanket around them, dense and filled with humidity.

'Okay, yes, I have financial obligations,' she finally confessed, because the whole story was going to be better than half a story. If she dropped it all, he would be left thinking that her parents were irresponsible layabouts who exploited her good nature, and just thinking that made her feel angry on their behalf.

'My parents have never been good about money and it's not because they're stupid or lazy. It's just that...' Her voice trailed off. She thought about her colourful childhood. Exciting, unpredictable, joyful...but what a learning curve in the end. And she thought about his: predictable, wealthy, privileged and with zero learning curves beyond how much more money it was possible to make.

'Just that what?'

And suddenly Erin felt her lips twitch and she looked at him with raised eyebrows and grinned.

What would her billionaire boss, who had always been protected from the hardships of life, who'd probably never glimpsed any life too far removed from the one he'd led, what would he think of hers?

Her smile broadened when he frowned and she could tell that he was bemused and disconcerted by her sudden change of attitude.

'Raffaele, this might come as a shock to you but until I was twelve, I grew up in a commune.'

Erin stifled a laugh when his mouth dropped open in shock. She'd shocked him once when she'd mentioned that her parents had a small holding and a tiny cottage industry…and now she'd shocked him again with this revelation.

'A commune…'

'It was wonderful, to be honest. I'm not sure how my parents drifted into that lifestyle but I think they'd both been hippies from the very beginning and commune life appealed to them once I came along, which was quite late in life for them. I think they spent so many years just enjoying one another and enjoying their wonderful nomadic life that they only decided at the very last minute that they'd quite like…well…me. A child. And along I came, at which point they joined a commune. We lived in the middle of nowhere but it was a vibrant community and we were all home-schooled.'

'Home-schooled…'

'You look a little dazed, Raffaele. Is this all too much for you? Should I get the smelling salts out?'

'Is that the sound of you being patronising?'

'I'm afraid it might be.'

'And then what? What happened after the commune life?'

He was leaning against the door, staring at her with

his long legs splayed and his hands loose between his thighs, which for some reason made her unexpectedly remember the sight of him in his boxers. Solid, muscled and way too sexy for his own good.

She quickly looked away.

Her brief flirtation with amusement at making him uncomfortable now felt dangerous.

'We travelled,' she said abruptly. Her voice softened with memories. 'I think my parents stuck it out being in one place when they had me but in the end, the wanderlust gene was too much. It was embedded way too deep in both of them. Maybe if one of them had wanted security, then life would have been different, but they were absolutely both on the same page.' She half closed her eyes and enjoyed the warm breeze blowing her hair this way and that. 'Unfortunately,' she said drily, twisting to look at him and noting that the dazed expression still hadn't quite left his face, 'travelling didn't come with the usual stuff like pensions and savings. They worked as they moved around, sometimes for a while in one place if it took their fancy but…'

'But then the time came for them to put down roots and they found that their… What did they do all this travelling in? Whatever it was, it wouldn't do as a permanent roof over their heads.'

Erin tried to take offence and bristle at that remark but found she couldn't, because there was clearly nothing malicious behind it. He sounded genuinely curious and interested.

'Actually, we changed homes several times.' She slanted a glance at him and smiled wryly. 'Almost like normal people moving house. When we left the commune, I remember a brightly painted mobile home and then an old four-wheel drive with a caravan. My dad could turn his hand to most things. He was really clever, and especially gifted with cars. Some of his jobs paid enormously well and we would hang around for a while, reaping the benefits. Sometimes we did actually stay put long enough for me to go to school somewhere, but we were never anywhere longer than a handful of months.'

'And how was that lifestyle for you?'

'Had its ups and had its downs.'

She looked at him seriously, establishing boundaries. No matter how much she was attracted to him, she still knew he was her boss—utterly off-limits—and it felt important to subtly manoeuvre the conversation so that he was aware of that. Just because some of the barriers between them had been eroded, she didn't want his finely attuned antennae picking up any signals that would set alarm bells ringing.

'It made me resilient, I think,' she mused thoughtfully, eyes half lowered but still keenly gauging his reaction to what she was telling him. He looked frankly fascinated and she felt a kick of something pleasing in that. 'It also made me really value the importance of financial security. Thank goodness for that, as things turned out. It also made me value even more the importance of...emotional security. My parents adore one another but for me love would have to be with a guy who was committed to settling down, in one place. A house with a picket fence and a couple of apple trees in the back garden.' She grinned. 'If you get my drift.'

'Sounds dull.' He grinned back at her. 'Sure there's

no longing for adventure waiting to break through the picture-perfect future you have all mapped out?'

'None,' Erin said firmly. She thought of him, yet again, in those boxers and sucked in a steadying breath. 'Absolutely none *whatsoever.*' She smiled blandly as they hit tarmac and the jeep picked up a bit more speed. 'Thanks for bringing me into town. I have an idea, why don't you look around the place while I grab a couple of things more suitable for the weather? I can meet you back in half an hour or so.'

Holding her bland, unrevealing gaze, Raffaele nodded and returned the smile with an equal measure of politeness. Underneath, though, he was burning to reject Erin's signature *hands off* change of topic and ask more. The little she had opened up and shown him had kick-started more questions than it had provided answers, and he was startled at just how urgently his wanted her to keep talking.

She'd told him that the women he dated were shopaholics who needed no urging to tell him all about themselves and she'd been right. He dated open books.

Honestly, that had always suited him. He had no interest in anything long term so if they liked to be indulged and if they enjoyed talking nonstop about themselves, then that had always been fine.

Now, he could feel his brain engage—in the presence, for the first time, of a woman who clearly didn't want to prolong the conversation and who had no interest in him beyond the fact that he was responsible for her pay cheque at the end of every month.

She'd said as much.

Hell, she didn't even *consider him a friend*!

Logic told him that in the face of all that, his best way forward was to drop all interest in trying to get to the bottom of her and return to the fault free, perfect working relationship they had always had.

Or he could pursue it.

Since when had he ever not been up for a challenge?

The week, he decided, was going to be a great deal more interesting than he could ever have imagined.

CHAPTER SIX

'THE TIMING WORKS WELL' was the first thing Raffaele said when they met back at the jeep an hour after their arrival in town. Erin had visited three boutiques, but she could have happily stayed longer: the settlement was compact, a picturesque collection of souvenir shops nudging against places where the locals shopped. Small grocery stores, a chemist, various shops selling fabric all rolled in huge bales and stacked like colourful sausages on counters inside the stores and on rickety tables outside to lure customers in.

'How so?'

Hand on the door, ready to hop in, Erin shaded her eyes and looked up at Raffaele.

He slung the bags of clothes she had bought into the back of the jeep and opened the door for her.

'A family friend who has a yacht moored on one of the islands just north of here is coincidentally around for two days. He's cruising along the chain of islands. My father knew I was here and got in touch with me to suggest a meeting. Something he wants me to discuss about a business the guy is thinking about expanding. The guy's a crashing bore and I could do without the hassle, but needs must. I've arranged to meet him for lunch on his yacht. Of course, you're more than welcome to join me but I'm guessing you'd rather return to the hotel? The pool is very nice.' He looked up at the blue skies, then returned his gaze to her. 'I'd be tempted myself if I had the chance.'

'I wouldn't dream of intruding on your lunch, Raffaele, though I don't for a minute think the man's a bore. If he's sailing along these islands, then he has to be interesting.'

'Your logic escapes me,' Raffaele murmured, his deep blue eyes roving over her flushed face. 'Just because someone has a boat and knows how to handle it, it doesn't make him interesting.'

'No,' Erin mused thoughtfully, 'I guess you're right. To be interesting, he really has to know how to chase a bat out of a room and claim to know how to deal with venomous snakes even though he might never have encountered one outside of a zoo.'

Raffaele threw his head back and burst out laughing.

'I always knew you were sharp, Erin,' he murmured when his full-bodied laughter had subsided, 'but your sense of humour still continues to surprise, especially now that you've released it from captivity.'

Erin's heart skipped a beat. She hurriedly broke eye contact and climbed into the rear of the jeep. The windows were all down and Raffaele leaned half into the car, looking at her.

'Sure you'll be okay?'

'Of course I will, Raffaele. I'll return to the hotel and have a lovely walk around and then, of course, I'll also do whatever work you want done. I'll check incoming emails and make sure nothing urgent needs sorting. I've already played truant going into town and missing our first meeting of the day.'

'Or you could just laze by the pool and forget about work.'

'That's not what I'm being paid to do.'

'I'm your boss, don't forget. If I say you can relax, then you can relax. Relax.'

'I'll certainly think about it. Oh, and before I forget, thank you for the Amex card and for…funding my change of clothes. There really was no need.'

'Erin, do you honestly think I would let you spend your hard-earned cash buying clothes for a week because yours weren't that suitable?'

'Maybe,' she said quietly, 'you might have if you didn't know about my parents, about the fact that I currently…lend a helping hand with their finances. Honestly, it's just until they can sort themselves out completely…' Their eyes met and she refused to look away. 'I don't want the little you know about my background to influence your behaviour towards me.'

'You underestimate me. But still, I can't put what you've told me about yourself to the side and pretend that it doesn't exist. It exists.'

Erin glanced away in receipt of this blunt truth. She had confided. She had told him things that would alter their relationship and now she could only hope it wasn't for the worse.

There was no going back. But she couldn't help but notice that whilst she had been encouraged to open up, he'd seen no such compulsion to return the favour.

Maybe on one occasion she'd sensed something about his background in the intonation of a throwaway remark… But her memory of that whole conversation before their flight was a muddle by now. She could have been mistaken.

She shrugged. 'What are the plans for the evening? Is anything arranged?'

'Funny you should ask. We're going to be meeting a few of the staff and their respective partners. It'll be an informal get-together so that we can try the food and I believe there might be some live music.'

She unconsciously made a face and he slanted her a slow, curling smile.

'Time for that box to be broken as well,' he purred silkily.

'What box?'

'The one you shut yourself in every time something like an informal get-together with good food and live music presents itself.'

'I don't do that!' Erin reddened. 'Can you name one instance when I've done that? I can't remember the last time I was at a party with live music!'

'My point exactly. That's just the sort of thing you should be throwing yourself into, instead of dreaming about picket fences and apple trees in the back garden with some guy you have yet to meet. Unless…' He lowered his voice and the smile was still there, this time a little broader. 'Unless you've already got him stashed away in a cupboard somewhere and you're going to tell me all about him at a later date? Produce him from thin air like a rabbit from a hat? You seem to be full of surprises of late.'

Erin ignored him. 'What time is this event happening, Raffaele, and where exactly? I'll meet you there.'

'Of course.' He grinned, drew back and gave her a half salute, although his deep blue eyes remained firmly fixed on her face. 'Six sharp in the meeting room in the main hotel. Someone from reception will take you through. I'd say I'd walk you over but I'm not entirely sure how long it will take me to get back after lunch with the bore. You might have to hold the fort for a bit, but you've done that before.'

'No problem.'

'Right then.' He slapped his hand on the side of the jeep, drew back and nodded to the driver. 'Off you go and Erin…don't work today. Have the day off. Gather your strength for the gruelling ordeal of the food and live music nightmare scenario.'

'I'm actually looking forward to it,' Erin purred, steely eyed. 'I really fancy immersing myself in the culture and getting to meet some new faces.'

'That's the spirit!'

The man, Erin thought as the jeep began bumping its way back to the hotel and away from the hot, tiny town, was insufferable.

Brilliant…sharp…edgy…challenging and stupidly good-looking, all of which combined probably explained the highly developed insufferability gene.

He expected her to show up, politely do what she had to do and then leave just as soon as was humanly possible. That was his impression of her in a relaxed environment. So she didn't really like work social dos! Since when was that a crime?

She did her absolute utmost to spend the rest of the day enjoying the hotel grounds, which were more extensive than she'd first thought.

She had some lunch in the same place where earlier she and Raffaele had had breakfast, chatted to some of the guests and then explored the untamed gardens. By midday, there were no thoughts of creepy-crawlies. The sun shone down with searing heat, making her feel lazy and lethargic and not at all in the mood for doing any work. She managed to find the waterfall, which was tucked away in a clearing. It was easy because she just had to follow the voices of a few of the guests enjoying the cool, refreshing water, and as she lingered at the side, watching them have fun, she wished she'd had the foresight to wear her swimsuit.

At the back of her mind, as she strolled through the forested grounds and explored the more cultivated gardens, a huge section of which was devoted to vegetables and beds of fresh herbs, the image of Raffaele lingered. She expected to bump into him at any given moment. The man had a habit of catching her unawares.

She didn't feel as horrifically exposed as she'd always imagined she would after sharing a slice of her private life with him, but she had made a decision. This was her chance to turn over a new leaf. The time had come to put her annoying crush on her boss to bed.

Now that she'd started down that road, it would be so easy to keep spilling little pieces of herself, to parcel out glimpses of her unusual background in the hopes it would win her scraps of surprise and amusement from her sexy boss. But unusual backgrounds didn't always make for anything interesting. Unless she changed her behaviour, she would always still be the sparrow who didn't know how to live life to the full, nursing an impossible crush instead of striking out in search of something real.

The sense of adventure that had swept through her when she'd stepped off the plane straight into the searing tropical heat swept through her again as she had a shower and relaxed and decided what she was going to wear for the meet-and-greet later on.

Why stick to her comfort zone? Here? In this amazing place that begged for her to live, for a moment, in a different skin…?

Raffaele made it back to the hotel with not much time to spare. He felt borderline traumatised by lunch with the bore who had droned on interminably about every single little setback that had befallen him and his wife on their six-week sailing tour of the Grenadines. Raffaele was sorely tempted to tell him that he should just pack it in because if he couldn't enjoy what everyone else would have given their right arm to do, then he didn't deserve the opportunity to do it.

He'd refrained but had spent several hours trying not to look at his watch too much and swatting away the man's wife.

Bridgette, blonde, leggy and all of thirty-four—thirty years younger than her rich husband—had greeted them at the yacht in a bikini and had spent the rest of her time surreptitiously trying it on with Raffaele.

It had been exhausting.

She'd reminded him a little of the women he was accustomed to dating, the same pouting physical perfection that expected attention from the opposite sex. But in this case, a wedding ring on her finger hadn't stood in the way of her relentlessly flirting.

The thought of seeing Erin, with her interesting background and her intelligent, cool, witty conversation, had had the call of the siren.

Now, as he shut the cabin door behind him to head to the hotel for the drinks party, he debated whether to knock on her door.

But no. He should leave her to it for now. Let her savour her time before the party. She was probably nervous. Strange place…unfamiliar faces…look at how spooked she'd been the night before when a bat had flown into the cabin! She hadn't yet settled into the vibe on this small tropical island. Her normal cool control was temporarily missing in action.

He liked the thought of holding her hand, metaphorically speaking, for the evening. If it came to discussing business, she would be brilliant as she always was, but he doubted there would be much of that.

There would also be a lot more people than originally planned. The modestly sized gathering had swollen to include friends and friends of friends and businessmen who all knew each other because the island was so small. Word of mouth had sent the numbers soaring.

She would be lost.

He idly savoured the pleasurable thought of swooping in as her knight in shining armour once again as he strolled unhurriedly towards the main hotel, which was lit up like a Christmas tree.

The place was much busier than it had been previously. Not only busy with the hotel guests, scant though their numbers were, but busy with people arriving in droves, laughing in groups.

He marvelled at the informality of it all. Back in the UK, no one would have ever contemplated tagging along to any party he threw unless there was an official invite. For starters, they would never have been able to bypass border patrol at his front door.

He spotted Gary, waved and cast one backward glance over his shoulder in the direction of the cabin where Erin was no doubt getting ready and maybe wondering whether she would fit in.

'A few more people than I'd anticipated.' He had to raise his voice as Gary fell into step with him. They entered the main hotel together, Raffaele towering over the smaller guy by at least ten inches and exuding the sort of lazy power that made people spin around to look at him with interest.

He was idly looking around. He reckoned there would be perhaps forty people there in total, excluding hotel guests who would be milling around but not allowed through to the various rooms where the informal get-together was being held.

He could hear the sound of music growing more insistent as they exited towards the back of the main hotel, out to a separate building which was used for functions.

Gary was telling him something about the function rooms. Weddings…anniversaries…private parties…not as popular as it could be…sometimes tourists in particular liked to have a beach on their doorstep…how could a beach compare to a rainforest…beaches were two a penny…every Caribbean island had one…

Raffaele was half listening.

He was busily searching the crowd when he spotted her. For a couple of seconds, his brain simply didn't register what his eyes were telling him.

Erin.

She was dancing! Since when did his well-mannered secretary dance? And she was dancing with a man…

Raffaele stopped dead in his tracks.

The room was cleverly lit. Sultry, shadowy nooks and crannies gave an atmosphere of intimacy, but it wasn't so dark that people couldn't see what they were doing. The crowd was lively, mostly young. On the edges, groups of older men and women were chatting. There was a space in the middle cleared for dancing and on a small rostrum, a trio of steel band players was rocking classic old tunes.

And there Erin was…*dancing.*

And here *he* was, hardly able to breathe as he watched her sway to the beat of the steel band without a scrap of inhibition. In the arms of some young, good-looking guy who was grinning like the cat that got the cream.

She was wearing something and nothing much: a bright yellow vest that clung to her slender body and emphasised her small, rounded breasts, and a flowered wrap-around skirt in shades of yellow and orange and bright green, slit up both sides so that her thighs were visible with every sinuous movement.

And where were her sensible shoes? All-weather and practical?

He remembered the pale pink toenails… Now the shoes she was wearing matched those pale pink toenails. They were tan gladiator-style sandals with beads.

Raffaele had no idea why he was so shocked by the vision of his secretary being twirled on a dance floor by a complete stranger, her head thrown back as she laughed with delight.

She was doing the very thing he had been encouraging her to do and yet…and yet…he wasn't sure he *liked* to see her in action. Of course he had *meant* every word he had said about her needing to relax, to just *let go*, but had she any real idea of how easy it was to give some young guy—and some young guy they didn't know from Adam—the wrong impression?

He realised his jaw was slack and quickly pulled himself together. Briskly, he walked towards her, only stopping when he was towering over her partner.

'Erin!'

Her cheeks were pink and her eyes were sparkling. She looked every inch the carefree girl he'd been imagining she could become when he'd encouraged her to step out of the box she liked to hide in. Although now he wondered whether he had got that completely wrong.

Maybe the box had only ever been for his benefit. Maybe this was the real Erin and she'd simply chosen not to show him.

He sensed that his smile was more of a scowl as he cut in, inserting himself between the couple just as the tempo changed from bouncy to cosy.

He slid his arms around Erin's waist and dipped down so that he was more on her level.

'Having fun?'

Erin felt the sinewy hardness of Raffaele's body against hers and everything in the room disappeared. Suddenly, it felt as though it was only the pair of them on a dance floor that had shrunk to the size of a postage stamp.

'I was,' she managed in a wry voice, edging back but finding that his hold was just slightly too tight to easily disengage.

He looked amazing in a pair of linen grey trousers,

loafers and a black polo shirt that fitted him like a glove. He hadn't shaved and his six-o'clock shadow was unforgivably sexy.

'Who's the kid?'

'Kid?'

'The one you were dancing with.'

'He's a year older than me so I'm not sure "kid" would be the right description, Raffaele.'

'Exchanged personal information already? Quick work.' His voice was light and amused.

Erin shrugged.

'I didn't expect to find you here before me,' Raffaele said, sweeping her towards the side of the room so that they were now on their own, away from the hubbub of people.

He stopped abruptly and stepped back to look at her with an expression, Erin noted, that looked a lot like disapproval.

She felt her hackles rise.

Did he imagine that he owned her? That because she'd shared something of herself with him, he could now dictate what she did while they were over here? Maybe he figured that an episode with an errant bat now warranted full protection just in case she had another Victorian-maiden-style meltdown over nothing.

'Why not?' she asked bluntly.

He looked away briefly and raked his fingers through his dark hair.

'I figured that you might have been a little…nervous. I did actually make an effort to get back here so that I could be by your side when you came over to the main hotel but everything just dragged on and on with Clive and his wife getting more and more inebriated over lunch until I finally managed to escape.'

'Oh dear. But wait...why do you think I might have been nervous? Didn't you say that I should head over here to meet and greet and get the lay of the land if you weren't around? Didn't you remind me that that was something I was accustomed to doing? So why would you think that I might have been nervous?'

'Because you're in unfamiliar territory... It can be daunting...'

Erin's hackles rose a little more but she wasn't going to be drawn into self-defence.

'We should be mingling,' she said coolly. 'If you like, I can see what business I can do but it doesn't seem the right place or the right time to try to introduce profit-and-loss discussions into the conversation.'

'Of course I don't want you to work!'

'Thank you. I'll get back to the party in that case?'

'Erin...'

'I'll be up first thing tomorrow morning, Raffaele, and I can meet you for breakfast at eight thirty if that suits.'

'You're overreacting...'

'To what exactly?' She sighed, banking down her annoyance, her impatience, her desire to give him a piece of her mind, because she didn't suddenly need her handsome boss thinking that he had to look out for her. 'Doesn't matter, Raffaele. Let's just drop all of this, could we? I guess we're both adjusting to being in a different country with different customs and—' she looked around her but had to grit her teeth to hide the resentment '—different scenery, not to mention the heat. Gets to a person if they're not used to it.'

She forced a smile. He didn't smile back and with a small shrug at his lack of response, she peeled off back to the party. Her dance partner seemed to be waiting for her, ready to pick up where they'd left off.

Left on his own, Raffaele scowled and stared at the pair of them through narrowed eyes.

Erin shimmered. The bright colours suited her, made her chestnut hair glow with different shades of auburn and brown, emphasised the gracefulness of her slender body and the slimness of her shapely legs.

She moved like a dancer.

Come to think of it, she'd always had that graceful way about her and he had always noticed it. He must have filed the observation away somewhere in his subconscious.

The rest of the evening was fun, lively, busy and he managed to work the room without being obvious.

He may have chatted with Erin a several times during the course of the evening, may have exchanged a couple of comments about the food, the music, the vibe, but whether he was talking to her not, he knew that he hadn't let her really out of his sight and she'd been in his head even when his attention seemed to have been one hundred percent focused on whoever he happened to be talking to.

The place was thinning out by ten and when Erin and the boy—Raffaele had discovered that his name was Thompson—began moving towards the door, Raffaele was hit with a surge of…fierce possessiveness that shook him.

He dumped his conversation with two women who

had managed to corner him and made for the door as well, intercepting Erin and Thompson just as they were about to head out.

'I'll take it from here,' he addressed the much slighter guy with a terse smile, while lightly resting his hand on Erin's arm. 'Our cabins are side by side. You're…?'

'Gary's my uncle.' Thompson smiled but his big, dark, liquid eyes were fighting to look away from Erin. 'I have a little sightseeing business. We do the coral reefs in glass-bottomed boats…'

'Great! Sure I'll get around to chatting with you sometime if this hotel sale goes ahead but in the meantime—'

'Raffaele…!'

Raffaele looked at Erin blandly, hand still on her arm.

'In the meantime,' he continued, returning his gaze to Thompson, who was beginning to get the hint and good-naturedly backing away from a potentially awkward situation, 'Erin and I are going to be wrapped up with work 24/7…'

'Sure, man!' He grinned, then looked at Erin and winked. 'You know where to find me,' he said, 'and I'd love to show you around our island, take you to have some real local food at one of the villages you probably would never get around to visiting…'

'I'll call…'

'I'll be waiting!'

Raffaele watched this little exchange with frowning displeasure and as soon as the other guy had been eaten up in the darkness outside, Erin turned to him, hands on her hips.

'What was *that* about?'

'Come again?'

'You know what I'm talking about, Raffaele!'

Heading back to the cabins, they soon left the thick of the departing crowd. The music had wound down and now the night noises were forming their own symphony. The sound of the crickets, the frogs and the screech owls mingled with the music of the brightly coloured birds they'd seen at breakfast, still singing mournful songs in the darkness.

There was a slight breeze but not enough to sweep away the heat and the humidity. The lanterns and fairy lights that had been strung between the trees for additional light sparkled against the inky blackness.

'Let's sit for a bit…'

'Sit?'

'We've barely spoken this evening. I'd like to get your thoughts on anything helpful you might have picked up… from any of the people there. You know how it is…music, alcohol loosens tongues…'

'Raffaele, surely that can wait until tomorrow? Especially,' she added with biting sarcasm, 'as I'm sure you'll have me working flat out 24/7, just in case I might be tempted to see Thompson.'

In the darkness, Raffaele flushed darkly. He felt edgy and restless and unwilling to cut short a conversation that he wanted to have without quite understanding why.

'I may have slightly over-egged the pudding on that front.'

He'd led her to one of the many benches scattered in little clearings in the forest for tourists to sit and appreciate the scenery and watched as she hesitated before sitting down.

'Why? Why would you over-egg the pudding? You

made such a song and dance of telling me that this *wasn't* going to be a work, work, work busman's holiday.'

'Because...'

Raffaele raked his fingers through this hair and hesitated as his normally very logical, very precise, analytical mind became fuzzy and soft focused.

'Believe it or not, while you're over here I feel that you're my responsibility,' he said gruffly.

'Your responsibility?'

'Call me a dinosaur.'

'I can think of other words,' Erin muttered under her breath.

'That guy you were flirting with...'

'I was *having a conversation with him,*' Erin corrected impatiently. 'I wasn't *flirting.*'

'He was all over you like a rash.'

'Raffaele, are you *jealous*?'

For a few seconds, the silence stretched like elastic between them and Erin felt her heart in her mouth, felt her pulse race with treacherous desire.

'Of course I'm not *jealous,*' Raffaele gritted. 'I've never been jealous in my entire life. Have I ever said anything to you that would indicate that I'm the sort of guy who gets jealous?' He laughed shortly. 'Just because I'm telling you that you should be careful, it doesn't mean that I'm jealous.'

'"Be careful"?'

He *was* jealous. Erin could sense it in her bones, somewhere deep inside her. She had no idea why. Did he think that she was his possession because over the years he had never known her to be distracted by another man? Have a social life? Because, from his perspective, her life was devoted to him?

Her blood boiled and yet there was a treacherous thrill in thinking of herself as his possession. She was a feminist through and through and had always been proud of her determination and her drive and her independence and yet…right now in the heat of the tropical night, excitement threaded through her veins like quicksilver.

'What do you think I should be careful about?' she queried. 'Did you think that Thompson might have made a pass at me and I wouldn't have known what to do about it? That it might have been another bat-flying-in-the-cabin scenario, demanding an urgent rescue from you?'

'Who knows?'

'Well, believe it or not, *I* know.'

'I wouldn't want you to find yourself in an awkward situation,' Raffaele said heavily, his voice laced with discomfort as she continued to look at him, steely eyed.

'Well, thank you very much for your concern, Raffaele. That said, it was misplaced.'

'I'm not sure you were aware of just how…how…'

'How what?'

'How beautiful you looked tonight, Erin. There wasn't a man in that room who wasn't staring at you.'

In the sultry heat, with the rustle of trees around them and the darkness turning everything into shadows and shifting angles, Erin stared at him and was ensnared by the glitter in his eyes.

Her heart skipped a beat.

She wondered whether she'd misheard what he had said. Was her mind playing tricks on her? Was she feverishly hallucinating that he had said the very thing she'd always imagined him saying in those wild fantasies she'd had about him?

'I… I…' she stammered. 'S-sorry? I'm not…uh… following you…'

'Okay, then I guess there's no harm in making it clearer. You looked amazing tonight, Erin. Stunning… beautiful…sexy. Any more descriptions you might need to get the picture? Every eye in that room was on you, including mine.'

The silence lengthened between them, stretched to breaking point.

'I could see what that guy wanted to do from a mile away. He wanted to touch what he was staring at. Maybe you didn't see that but I did. He wanted to do…exactly what I wanted to do…'

CHAPTER SEVEN

RAFFAELE HAD NEVER found himself in a position where he was making a pass at a woman without being absolutely certain that it would be a reciprocal situation. In actual fact, women were often the ones who did the pass-making, with him in the role of obliging recipient.

But that was what he had just done, wasn't it? Made a pass at Erin? She was staring at him in dumbfounded silence and he couldn't blame her.

If *he* couldn't understand what had just happened there, then what were the chances that she would? Had telepathy ever been one of her many skills?

He stared back at her, gauging her reaction in the steamy darkness and utter silence.

He should have been kicking himself but he wasn't. In fact it was a struggle not to reach out and do what his body wanted: reach out and trail his finger over her lips and then bring his mouth to hers so that he could taste her.

Sex. Lust. Desire. A place he'd never thought he would ever want to explore with Erin Fisher, but right now it was the only thing he wanted. The alluring pull of the woman who made him laugh and made him think had collided with the intense drag of attraction, one that had roared into life with sudden, blinding ferocity when he'd seen her dancing.

'It's late,' he said abruptly. He stood up and remained standing as she stumbled to her feet.

Erin took a step back from him, desperate to put some distance between them because what he had just said was ringing in her ears. *He thought she was sexy? Beautiful? Since when? Had she failed to notice that pigs had started flying?*

'It's late, yes,' she said feebly, 'and I'm guessing that you must have had more to drink than you imagine. That rum punch was really strong.'

But even as she spoke, the glittering intent in his eyes had her spellbound.

'I never drink more than I should. Do you think I must have had too much to drink because of what I've just said to you?'

'Yes, if you really want to know.'

'Why wouldn't I find you sexy? Beautiful?'

'Because...'

'Because...?'

'Because I don't think that this conversation is appropriate.'

'That's not an answer. Give me an answer.'

'Oh, for goodness' sake! Because that's not the sort of thing that's ever happened to me!' Erin burst out in a rush. 'Satisfied?'

'No.'

'What do you mean by that? What do you mean by *no*? You can't say that.'

'You fascinate me, Erin Fisher, which is why I want to find out more about you. And yes I can say it. I just did.'

They stared at one another.

When he reached out to trace the outline of her jaw, she audibly gasped but the thrill of his touch was… electric. It turned every bone in her body to jelly. She wanted to subside right back onto the bench but weirdly, she was incapable of any movement at all. She could only stare at his beautiful face, cast in shadows. That feathery touch had come and gone in seconds but the heat from his finger lingered, and she had to resist the temptation to cover the spot with her hand.

She longed to touch him back. Yearned for it and yet the awareness of the danger of going there roared through her with the force of a volcano.

This was a risk she couldn't take. *Wouldn't take*. She wanted love and this road led to…despair. She knew this man, knew herself…knew the two should never, ever merge.

'Since when do I fascinate you, Raffaele?' she scoffed weakly.

He shrugged and looked up to the dark, cloudless sky, the hundreds of thousands of stars studding it, then gazed at her thoughtfully for a couple of seconds.

'I don't know and you're right. Ridiculous conversation. You don't have to answer anything.' He smiled crookedly. 'Sometimes curiosity gets the better of me and yes, add to that that I happen to find you sexy and it's a combustible mix. You go back to your cabin. I'm going to remain out here for a bit…get my thoughts in order.'

Faced with a choice, Erin dithered, watched as he sat back down, stretching his long legs in front of him.

This was about as exciting as life had got for her in… in as far back as she could remember.

She'd played it safe. She always had. With her love life, with her work life, with her plans for her future. As she'd learned from her parents, choosing not to walk the straight and narrow might lead to adventure, but there were too many downsides for it to ever appeal to her.

But now, under a velvety black sky studded with a million stars and the man who'd featured in too many of her fantasies over the years… She could barely breathe as excitement reared its head, beckoning her to explore.

Somehow she found herself sitting on the bench next to him. Succumbing to something more powerful than all her internal back-and-forth reasoning.

'I work for you.' She turned to him and heard the pleading in her voice.

'I get that and like I said, you don't have to indulge me.'

'This is just a simple conversation.' *Was it?* 'I suppose I've been working for you for quite some time so it's only natural we end up sharing a little more than just the superficial stuff… No big deal.' The steamy, sultry air made her lazy, challenged her to step out of her comfort zone for once in her life even though she continued to tell herself that a conversation was just…a conversation.

She sighed into the stretching silence. 'My life…on the road so much of the time…it was difficult to form friendships, to form relationships. My mum and dad only ever saw it all as a huge adventure but really, for me, my most secure time was when we were at the commune and things were the same every day. I missed that when we took to the road. I missed the routine, I missed the sameness. I missed the faces that would be there every morning when I woke up and every evening before I went to bed, and those times when we settled for a bit… when I managed to go to school…it was hard. The other kids… You know kids, they can be cruel. They sometimes laughed at us, called us names. That said, there were a lot of amazing times, a lot of friendly faces but even so…' She turned away, mortified at her outburst but when she moved to stand up, he stayed her with his hand.

'Keep talking, Erin.'

His voice was low and serious, the voice *of a friend.* Except he wasn't a friend, was he? Or if he was, then this was no longer an innocent friendship. A Pandora's box had been opened and she was struggling to put the lid back on it. Her head was saying one thing but her body was exerting a power that was too strong.

'What else is there to talk about?' Erin breathed in deeply at the memories of her younger years. 'Is this all information overload? I'm guessing you don't have a lot of stamina for women pouring their hearts out to you.'

Raffaele was caught up in a moment he couldn't have foreseen in a thousand years.

Frankly, she was right about his usual appetite for heart-to-hearts. Zero. But right now, right here, she could have kept talking forever because he wanted to keep listening forever.

'Besides,' she chided good-naturedly, 'I notice I'm the only one doing the talking.' Another laugh. 'Fine by me but I think I'll call it a day now before you start thinking that you have to fish around to find a hankie to mop up my tears.'

'Confiding…doesn't come easily to me…' Raffaele said roughly.

'Doesn't to me either, it has to be said. Just another one of those things learned along the way. You never really get the time needed to build the sort of friendships that encourage girlish confidences.' She shrugged but her voice was sad. 'So you learn to keep things to yourself. You don't have to share anything with me. In fact, it's a good idea if you don't. I've already said too much.'

'You think my life was perfect,' Raffaele said on a wrenched sigh and then was astonished. He hadn't meant to say anything about himself. That was the program he'd always stuck to.

'No one's life is perfect but some of us have a bit more to contend with.' Erin smiled kindly.

'Fair enough.' He smiled back at her crookedly. 'I didn't live on the road, travelling wherever the wind happened to blow. I wasn't isolated from my own peer group because I never stayed in the same place long enough to establish a base but…'

'But?'

Raffaele peered forward into the unknown, into the possibility of handing himself over to someone else. His early-warning systems were ringing in his ears but he wanted to ignore them.

It felt like an act of wild courage.

When he looked at Erin, her head was tilted to one side and her expression was curious but gentle.

Maybe if he'd seen anything else but that gentle curiosity he wouldn't have taken a deep breath and said, 'My parents have a loveless marriage. It was always a union that made sense between two powerful families, but love? No. I barely saw them. I was sent to boarding school almost as soon as I was out of nappies. Maybe if I'd been around them I would have stopped hoping for a show of affection that was never going to come a bit earlier than I did. But I just kept on hoping, until I didn't. Eventually, I wised up to my place in the pecking order.' He shrugged. 'I was a teenager when I discovered my father's affair.' He laughed shortly. 'Why it came as such a shock I have no idea but it did.'

'How awful for you.'

'These things happen. Their marriage weathered it, though. I later found out that their marriage had, in fact, weathered my father's *numerous* affairs. My mother told me when I asked her. She didn't really see why it mattered. Their marriage was everything a marriage should never be, held together because neither of them wanted to abandon their precious status quo.'

'That's a dreadful learning curve for anyone, far less a vulnerable adolescent. Raffaele, I'm so sorry. That must have been devastating for you. We look to our parents to define the road we'll end up travelling down, at least emotionally.'

'I handled it.' He raised his eyebrows, forcing his expression to resume its usual cool. 'You know why I don't get wrapped up in relationships that lead anywhere? Because I learned that I wasn't capable of it… I can do *sex* better than most but love is something I have no interest in. Like you say…the road I have ended up travelling down was defined for me by my distant parents in their loveless union.' He laughed mirthlessly. 'I have no idea why I've just told you that but…' He shrugged indifferently. 'Learning curves are wonderful things.

I know mine have made me as tough as nails. Handy when it comes to doing business.'

But not, Erin thought, her heart constricting, *when it comes to anything else*. He had retreated from that window of vulnerability and she knew better than to try to continue the conversation.

He had let her in briefly and now the door would be shut. But she'd had a striking glimpse of a guy who would never commit to loving anyone when the example set had been devastating for him.

'I should head in.' She stood up and feigned a yawn. He stood as well, towering over her and giving her hammering heart no respite.

'Have a drink with me. In my cabin. Or yours.'

'A *drink*?'

'It's a thing, I hear. Some call it *a nightcap*.'

She hesitated. Part of her wanted to do just that, to have a drink with him, but then she shook her head briskly. Immediately, he backed off, raising both hands in a gesture of amicable surrender.

'Until the morning, in that case.' He spun around on his heels and began heading towards their cabins. She fell in alongside him, still unsettled.

'And the plans are? I mean for tomorrow?'

Raffaele answered readily enough, and Erin could tell that he was as relieved as her to dive into the details of the meetings they had lined up tomorrow. After whatever rogue impulse that had propelling him into opening up to her, talking about work was a return to known terrain, a safe and comfortable refuge.

But then they were standing outside her cabin, and his eyes drifted to her.

'It'll be a hot day,' he murmured as she inserted the key. 'Dress as light as you can and wear a swimsuit under your clothes. The waterfall will be on the menu and it'll look very strange if you hang back.'

Erin quailed.

After everything that had happened tonight…how he had looked at her tonight, that he had told her she was sexy, the way her senses had been roused… And even more dangerous than that, that shared moment between them when the world had stood still…

After all that, the thought of parading around in a swimsuit was unsettling. But if she were to be successful in moving on from tonight's revelations, then she would have to act as though it didn't matter. And the swimsuit she had brought with her was the last word in prim. If he'd suddenly found her sexy in her new-found peacock clothes, then he'd soon be catapulted back to square one the second he spotted her in her black one-piece. That was some consolation.

If he never mentioned those low, murmured confidences again, she would be happy to pretend that they didn't exist. Things would settle back into place with maybe just the odd jarring reminder here and there.

'I wouldn't dream of hanging back.' She lightened the mood with a cheery laugh. Something wicked stirred inside her. 'For starters, Thompson would never forgive me if he's there! See you in the morning, Raffaele!'

To Raffaele's intense annoyance, he found himself spending the following day of meetings and socialising on high alert for the Thompson kid. He didn't sit on the managerial board of the hotel, so should if Thompson appeared, then obviously Raffaele would be within his rights to send him on his way. Very satisfying to savour the thought of that.

He also found himself surreptitiously watching out for signs of flirting from the team, most of whom were young.

Erin had shown up for work very modestly dressed in some neat, soft navy cotton shorts, a daffodil-yellow T-shirt and some flat tan sandals. But somehow she still managed to look as tempting as she had the night before in her brightly coloured outfit. It felt as though a thought had taken root in Raffaele's head, and now that it had, it was intent on sprouting all sorts of tendrils.

She had also reverted to her usual polite self, controlled, smiling and helpful. He should have welcomed that. He didn't. He wasn't going to return to any of the touchy-feely, kumbaya nonsense he'd strayed into last night. But he also wasn't going to pretend that he wasn't aware of her as a woman either.

Last night he'd done nothing but think of her until finally, unable to sleep, he'd got up and worked. Or at least tried to.

Thoughts of her had driven him mad. The things he'd told her…the things she'd told him…the way their eyes had locked together, two people trying hard to fight the obvious.

All he could see in his mind was her. As a man to whom the adulation of women had always been a given, he simply hadn't known how to handle the one woman who eluded him.

He had always had a policy of never actively pursuing any woman. At the end of the day, there were plenty of fish in the sea. But after a couple of hours of fitful sleep he had awoken to the realisation that that particular policy no longer held true.

There was only one fish in this ocean and that was the only fish he wanted.

God, he wanted her so much, as if a dam of dark, desperate want had been swirling under the surface for a million years and had now, finally, burst.

The intensity of what he felt didn't disconcert him at all.

When it came to women and his lack of faith in long-term relationships, there was always an underlying unease that they might end up wanting more than he would be prepared to give them. He always came clean from the start that he wasn't in it for marriage but even so…

Well, just look at Alexa and how that had turned out. She had ignored his warning completely.

With Erin, however, there would be no such fear. She knew him in a way no other woman did; she knew how he felt about longevity in relationships. The things he'd shared with her would only have reinforced what she would already have known. Love wasn't on his agenda and never would be. He could keep it physical, just like he kept all his relationships with women physical. That was a given.

More than that, when it came to a life partner, he simply wasn't her type.

In an ideal world, a fling on the other side of the world would be something they could both indulge in and then, once it was over, lock away in a box never again to be revisited. Their working relationship would resume the peaceful course it had once taken.

This wasn't an ideal world, of course, but Raffaele still thought they could navigate this situation. He had the perfect solution.

It was something he had been vaguely thinking about for a while. And now that their circumstances had changed, that vague thought had crystallised. It was waiting to be pulled out of the hat, magician style.

'Hope you're wearing your swimsuit,' he had murmured to Erin during their lunch break, as they stood at the buffet bar helping themselves to some of the delicious local food. 'As soon as the next round of meetings comes to an end, off we all go to sample the local beauty spots.'

'Of course I'm wearing my swimsuit!' She had looked at him with astonishment. 'Isn't that what you asked me to do? Or have you forgotten?'

Now, lunch done and the final meeting wrapped up, Raffaele stretched back in his chair and looked around at the eight men and women assembled at the table with him.

They were an efficient bunch. They all knew their numbers and even though they'd all been fully cognizant that the hotel had been gradually being sidelined by its current owner, they'd all maintained their enthusiasm to see it do as best as it could, given the financial restraints they'd been dealing with for the past couple of years.

'Okay.' Raffaele stood up and strolled through the boardroom, all eyes on him. 'Good work and I want to say that if I go ahead with this purchase, you'll all be in line for generous remunerations. You've been loyal to this hotel despite the fact that not a huge amount of money's been poured into it over the past two years.'

He paused behind Erin's chair and rested both hands on the back of it.

Automatically, Erin stiffened, feeling his presence behind her and reacting to it with every fibre in her being.

Playing it cool had taken everything out of her.

She'd barely slept the night before. Her head was stuffed full of images of her boss's dark, handsome face, that curling smile, the lazy intent in his eyes that challenged her to step out of the box and explore the unimaginable, those whispered words about the troubled boy behind the controlled man…

She realised she was holding her breath when she felt him straighten behind her and stroll away until he was standing at the head of the conference table, gazing at them. Only then could she breathe out.

'So I think I've done all my due diligence.' He moved to perch on the edge of the boardroom table. He was so mesmerising, so exquisitely good-looking that it felt as though everyone else there was also holding their breath waiting for him to finish talking. 'I have all my facts and figures so thank you all for your cooperation. No need to extend your hospitality further. Erin and I will now do a little exploring of the area on our own.'

Erin's mouth dropped open.

He caught her eye and his eyebrows shot up, feigning innocent surprise at her expression. 'We've already been to the town but there are a couple of beaches, I've been told, which are only accessible by boat…?'

Voices faded to a blur.

She was doing her best not to look appalled but wasn't sure what sort of job she was making of that.

She knew that at some point she was standing up, shaking hands with lots of the people there, making smiling noises about seeing them all again before she and Raffaele headed back to London.

When the door to the conference room was opened and people started filing out, she felt the blast of hot air rush in, cutting through the cool of the air conditioning.

Then the door shut, and she and Raffaele were alone in the room.

'They've worked hard,' Raffaele said. 'They don't need to keep disrupting their timetables to entertain us.' Erin looked at him, her expression carefully guarded, as he walked slowly towards her. 'I'd…like to have a chat with you, Erin.'

'What about?'

'Can't be summed up in one word. It's something of a spectrum.'

'I have no idea what you mean by that. Should I be concerned?' She laughed nervously and stared up at him.

'I guess it's a wait-and-see scenario.'

Erin kept a polite, curious smile pinned to her face but her heart was beating wildly as a million unpleasant outcomes raced through her head.

Top of the list was the sinking dread that he had somehow sensed her attraction to him and had been spooked by it. He might enjoy a bit of light flirtation here, in a place that was alien to both of them, but was he now backing away at speed from the terrifying possibility that she might be yet another woman greedy for love and commitment? Especially after what he'd shared with her?

All her insecurities rose to the surface with suffocating urgency.

She'd told him so much about herself and now she felt trapped by those unwitting confidences as though he could read her soul by putting together the path of breadcrumbs she had laid down. As though he could just *see* that his idea of light flirtation with the secretary he now knew a little more about had provoked a disproportionate, inappropriate reaction within her.

'How I love wait-and-see scenarios,' she said with an attempt at her usual dry humour and he obligingly smiled.

'Why don't we take a walk? We can head in the direction of the waterfall. It's probably quiet out there at this hour. People taking it easy after a day in the sweltering sun.'

'Sure.'

It was cooler than it had been, with rain in the air. Still steaming hot, though, and here, without any pretty lanterns and fairy lights, the forest around them felt wilder and lusher.

There was no one on the path they took. No locals, no tourists. They walked through a shadowy twilight semi-darkness under the canopy of trees with the squish of fallen leaves underfoot. Occasionally the fading sun would penetrate the canopy, sending shards of pale light through the branches of the trees. After a handful of minutes, during which they had walked in silence, they emerged into a glorious clearing where the waterfall, not very big at all, crashed over dark rocks into a crystal clear pool empty of people.

Erin walked down to the water, mesmerised by the

thunderous sound of the falls and the way they cascaded down, rippling outwards until the turmoil gave way to ice-cold water as still as a swimming pool.

She felt Raffaele next to her and her whole body stiffened with tension.

'Spit it out, Raffaele,' she stated as she spun around to face him. 'The suspense is killing me.'

'I want you.'

'Sorry?' She twisted to look at him but he continued staring out at the water, his jaw clenched.

'I want to sleep with you, Erin.'

'What? Wait. What are you saying? No!' Her voice shook. 'That can't happen!'

'Because you don't want to sleep *with me*?'

'I don't want to have this conversation. How on earth would we ever be able to carry on working together if we…if we…?'

This time he did face her and Erin's pulse raced at the absolute seriousness on his face. The very face she had longed to touch for so many years.

Her lips parted and her treacherous body took a step towards him. She saw just the ghost of a smile on his face. It should have been a signal for her to break the electric connection between them, but she couldn't.

He wanted her.

No misreading of signals, no imagination playing tricks on her. *He wanted her and she wanted him right back.*

She knew the dangers. She'd listed each and every one in her head a million times but crushing desire made a nonsense of all those rational concerns. Crushing desire was already making an argument for doing exactly what they both wanted, was telling her that this was just lust, that lust couldn't end up hurting her or derailing her hope of finding love with the right guy.

She trembled, her breath hitching, as Raffaele lowered his head, and the cool feeling of his lips on hers kick-started a cyclone of pent-up arousal inside her. She moaned into his mouth and stepped closer to him, her slender body pressed against his hard, masculine, much bigger one. She reached up and sifted her fingers through his dark hair as he continued to send her senses into spinning meltdown, first with his mouth, his invading tongue lashing against hers, and then with his hand, moving underneath her top and finding the cup of the swimsuit she'd worn under her clothes.

'This is too much,' he growled. 'We have to get a room.'

'Raffaele…'

'Come… I know where we can go… Jesus, I've never felt so turned on in my life before… I can barely get my thoughts together…'

Erin followed him blindly. He was saying something about the ledge he'd found behind the waterfall when he'd been on one of his earlier journeys of discovery.

The noise of the waterfall thundered around them. Sure-footed and agile, he held her hand as he led the way to the smooth, cool ledge behind the falls, big enough to sit and have a picnic with friends. Hidden from view by the wall of water a mere handful of feet away.

This was peace, privacy, a cool, misty respite from the stifling humidity.

There was nothing cool between them, though. Erin was burning up.

Her clothes were sticking to her like glue.

She began stripping off. Part of her could scarcely believe this was happening. Another part revelled in it, revelled in the freedom of being reckless for the first time in her life.

The ledge, smooth and flat, should have been uncomfortable, but it was lovely and slippery and cold underfoot. Erin found herself wondering how many couples had sneaked behind this waterfall over the decades to do exactly what they were doing now.

They didn't speak. The sound of cascading water feet away from them would have drowned out their voices anyway.

Erin liked it that way because she just wanted to feast her eyes on Raffaele and enjoy him in perfect, blissful silence.

When the last of his clothing was off, her mouth fell open. He'd worn swimming trunks underneath, black and navy blue, and as he kicked them to the side, to join the rest of his discarded clothes, she breathed in sharply and trembled.

He was impressive and there was no mistaking the fact that he was turned on.

She had begun undressing already. Now she couldn't wait to get her clothes off completely. She scrabbled at them while he stood exactly where he was, watching her with his hand resting idly on his erection.

She had never been so turned on.

He walked towards her and then held her. Their bodies glistened with perspiration and spray from the waterfall. She could smell the humid air and the scent of earth.

It felt as though time stood still as he began touching her, exploring her nakedness slowly with his hands while he kissed her. She had to reach up to him, half on tiptoe, her hands wound around his neck so that she could pull him tighter towards her.

Her breasts pressed against his hard chest. She felt the scrape of his hair against her nipples and rubbed herself against him so that the sensation was amplified.

He cupped her rounded bottom and massaged it, ran his hands along her waist and felt her shiver and then curved them around her breasts, inching slightly away from her so that he could rub the stiffened peaks of her nipples with the abrasive pads of his thumbs.

'I don't want to rush this,' he groaned. 'Would you rather we take this to a bed in one of our cabins? Although I'm not sure I can make it that far…'

'I want to stay here.'

'Then let me spread some of clothes out… We can lie down…'

It took Raffaele seconds to haphazardly spread some of their clothing in a reasonably good semblance of a sheet, but it felt like hours. Finally, it was done and they were staring at one another across the tumble of clothes on the ground.

Naked. With the spray from the waterfall on them and the cool of the grotto on them.

They moved towards one another in unison, eyes locked.

'I want to take this slowly,' he breathed into her ear, wrapping his arms around her in a caress that was almost chaste. 'I've been thinking about this…wanting it… wanting *you*… I want to take my time and pleasure you until you want me to carry on forever…'

Forever...? The word lingered in Erin's head, pernicious and heady, until she dismissed it because she wondered whether that was a word Raffaele would ever really understand.

They lay down together, adjusting their bodies until they found their comfort zone and then they began to explore one another.

Tentative…eager…slowly…hungrily…

They clung and kissed, at first urgently, limbs tangling but then the kiss softened as they tasted one another, neither wanting to break apart but both eager to explore more, to touch more.

Raffaele had never felt anything like this, anything so wild and powerful and consuming. Each time Erin whimpered, he had to steel himself against rushing everything because all he wanted to do was to reach his orgasm as fast as he could.

Every tiny movement she made against him sent his senses reeling.

He cupped her small breast in his hand as he trailed kisses along her neck and when she arched back, he obligingly took her pert nipple into his mouth and sucked hard on it.

She was so slim that he could feel the outline of her ribs under his hand, could feel every thrilling response to what he was doing, every small shudder.

He touched her lightly, ran his fingers in a feathery motion over her stomach as she sucked in her breath and then he dipped his fingers into her, into her wetness, feeling a slippery way to touch the spot that made her groan and begin to buck against his hand.

'We can't take this where I want to take it,' he groaned with anguished frustration, even as he continued to tease her, tickling the stiffened bud of her clitoris and feeling it pulse to his touch.

He briefly propped himself up to look down at her flushed face.

'Don't stop.'

'I don't have protection with me.'

'Arghh!' Erin likewise propped herself up on her elbows, her chestnut hair tumbling around her face, her mouth parted with desire. She pushed her hair from her face and stared at him. 'And I'm not on any contraception.'

'Wouldn't matter. I always make sure to be responsible for my own protection. You're beautiful, Erin.' He smiled when she blushed. 'Never mind. I know a million other ways we can satisfy one another and when we get back to my cabin…we can pick up where we left off. Might be fun to have some delayed gratification.'

'Says the guy who's probably never had to experience that in his life before?' she teased huskily.

He smiled back at her, appreciatively, eyes devouring her. 'Change is as good as a rest… I'm certainly finding the idea of delayed gratification a big turn-on.'

He stopped talking and began exploring, this time with his mouth and his tongue. He pushed her thighs apart and smelled her musky scent as he delicately licked her.

When she trembled, he could feel something intensely and gratifyingly masculine tear through him, a feeling of powerful possessiveness.

The thought that this was his prim and proper secretary was a turn-on like nothing else he'd ever experienced in his life before.

He stroked her thighs as he continued to tease her clitoris and then when he knew that she could no longer fight the surging, pulsing need to come, he thrust his fingers into her so that he could pleasure her with more than just his mouth.

Erin was taken to Heaven and back.

She arched back, detached from everything around her, lost in sensation, barely recognising her own guttural moaning as she came against his mouth.

The wall of cascading water cocooned them. It made the experience feel unreal and yet incredibly erotic.

Outside, the fading sun threw everything in that intensely private space into misty twilight.

It was surreal.

The noise of the waterfall…the humidity…the spectral light…and, as Erin surfaced back to reality, this glorious, beautiful man who had only ever existed for her like this in her deepest, darkest dreams.

She touched him all over, the way he'd touched her. Every bit of his naked body was a revelation and a delight.

She explored him, eyes open so that she could see what she was touching. She lost herself in the feel of him, hard and muscled under her exploring fingers. When she licked her fingers and gently stroked his flat, brown nipples, she thrilled to the way he shuddered and then gripped her hand, guiding it to his erection because he couldn't stand being teased any longer.

She enjoyed him the way he had enjoyed her, and

loved pleasuring him the way he had loved pleasuring her.

She had no idea where this freewheeling sense of freedom was coming from. Maybe because for the first time in her life, she was giving herself permission to do exactly what she wanted without counting the cost.

She was expunging the crush she had had on him for such a long time. She had never foreseen any of this happening but he had extended his hand. She had taken it without thinking about repercussions because, at least on the emotional front, she was safe.

He was a commitment-phobe. He could never be the sort of guy she would ever contemplate being a lasting feature in her life.

On a work front… Well, that posed a number of thorny issues, but for the moment, Erin decided that she would delay thinking about that.

There was a cabin to get to. There was hot, steamy, wonderful, wild, taboo sex on the menu…

Thorny issues were for another day.

CHAPTER EIGHT

'MY PARENTS WOULD give their eye teeth to see what I'm seeing right now.' Erin was lying on a lounger, looking out at a sunset that lit up the clouds in tones of sherbet. A soft, impressionistic swirl of orange, pink and lavender was rapidly being swallowed up by a star-studded, velvet blackness.

Raffaele's lounger was right next to hers and she felt his hand move to lightly rest on her stomach.

The yacht they'd rented four days previously was bobbing gently beneath them to the rhythmic lull of the waves lapping against the sides of the hull. They were both lying on their backs, looking at the same sunset, the same expanse of sky and the same calm ocean all around.

'Do they know you're here?' Raffaele asked curiously.

'Of course not.' Erin wriggled onto her side so that she could look at Raffaele. He was naked. Completely naked. So was she. They were miles from any of the islands that made up the Grenadines. If she peered through the gathering darkness, she might just be able to make out the silhouette of Bequia, where they had spent most of the day, but from here?

Just the ocean all around them. She could smell the salt from the sea. The horizon seemed to stretch forever.

It was dreamlike. A bit like everything that was happening between her and Raffaele. Dreamlike. She didn't want to wake up.

'You haven't told them that you're having a fling with your boss?'

Erin heard the smile in his voice and shivered.

'Of course I haven't.'

'Think they'd disapprove?'

'I know they would.'

'Why?'

Raffaele shifted so that he was lying on his side, looking at her. He ran his hand gently along her side, feathered over the dip of her waist and then stroked her flank until the usual responses were firing up.

Lust…desire…the spreading wetness between her thighs that longed for his touch, for his mouth…for the hard thrust of him inside her, filling her up.

Her breath hitched and she saw his eyes darken as he recognised what he was doing to her.

It was definitely a two-way street. She could see exactly what she was doing to him as well.

She felt languid. She wanted to be teased. She wanted to tease him. To talk while they touched one another.

'Oh, you know…'

'They disapprove of intra-office relationships?'

'They'd disapprove of me doing this…just having sex without any commitment…' She mirrored his stroking, running her hand along his thigh and liking the abrasive feel of hair-roughened, muscled skin.

He was fully erect and she teased the tip of his erection with her finger and smiled when he shuddered and clasped his hand over hers for a couple of seconds.

'From what you've told me about them, I'll admit I got the idea that they might have been a little more liberal in their thinking.'

'Because they led an unconventional lifestyle?' Erin thought about her parents, still crazily in love with one another. 'They were soulmates. They literally only had eyes for one another. They had me later in life but honestly… they're great believers in the power of love and all they've ever wanted for me was to find my own soulmate.' Erin hesitated. She'd told him a lot, but she hadn't mentioned David, the guy she'd dated, the mistake she'd made. 'Especially after David.'

'Who was David?'

Erin flopped back onto the lounger and stared off into the distance. Darkness had roared in, extinguishing the russet colours of sunset.

'Oh, he's someone I thought was the real deal. I was inexperienced. I built castles in the sky.' She smiled. 'It was never the real deal. We were never a match and when we broke up, he said some pretty harsh things…' She sighed. 'I got over him and it didn't take long to realise that he was toxic, passive-aggressive a lot of the time… moody when he didn't get his own way. I don't think I was really myself when I was with him and never relaxed into the relationship. I was in love with the thought of being in love so decided that it was okay to ignore red flags. When we broke up, he was pretty callous, pretty scathing about me and that hurt. A lot. So while that break-up was the best thing that could have happened to me in retrospect, I think it made my parents realise, and me as well, that the next relationship should be something healthy, a relationship with a future. My parents might have been hippies and still are, to be honest, but they'd see this as me wasting my time.'

'And do you? Think that you're wasting your time with me?'

The conversation was suddenly very serious. Thoughts that Erin had barely voiced to herself now rose to the surface.

Where was this going? How had that bridge to be crossed at some point in the future suddenly materialised under her feet? Was it because feelings she had dismissed as no more than a trivial crush were turning out to be something a lot more dangerous?

Her heart picked up pace.

Was she falling in love with a guy whose only commitment to her had been to take a few days off work? All so that they could prolong their time in this little bubble where reality could be suspended?

Raffaele hadn't even discussed what would happen when their time on this yacht was at an end!

And she'd just gone along for the ride because he was addictive. She'd squashed all her qualms when they'd tried to nudge through and told herself that she was in control. And why had she done that?

Because she loved him.

And the alternative of stepping back and taking stock was inconceivable, so she'd pretended there was no need to look beyond the moment. She'd dumped every principle she'd had when it came to men, lock, stock and barrel.

And now she was terrified.

Her mouth suddenly felt dry. 'Why would I think that?' she managed to say.

'Well, it sounds as though after the break-up, you programmed yourself to think that the only way forward would be with a guy with an engagement ring in his back pocket.'

His voice was light and amused but Erin thought she could pick up something in his voice, a wariness, the cautious testing of the ground. The hint of unspoken questions. *Was his secretary beginning to get unrealistic ideas about what they had? Which was, essentially, nothing? Should he be worried?*

It wasn't as though he'd said anything about a future… no plans beyond how they would occupy the next hour or so…

'Programmes have a way of changing,' Erin mused thoughtfully, absently, while her heart beat fast and wild against her ribcage. 'Your programme also changed, didn't it? But here we are.' She shrugged and smiled and then provocatively traced a line with her finger along his arm. 'I reckon this is just what I need. Something temporary…a fun stepping stone to the committed relationship I really want. I mean, I fell into the habit of taking time out from guys after my break-up. It was easy and it was lazy and I'm honest enough to admit that.' She smiled ruefully, something in her chest aching.

She loved this man... How could she have let this happen?

'"A fun stepping stone…"'

'That's it. A wonderful game. Wouldn't you agree? I mean, neither of us saw this coming and now we're here, it's almost as though we're not actually in the real world.'

'I can agree with that.' Raffaele smiled, trying to cover over the unsettling realisation that it was pretty much the only thing Erin had said that he was inclined to agree with.

Wrong. He could theoretically agree with all of it. He just didn't *like* every word he'd just heard.

A stepping stone? A bit of fun? Before she found Mr Right?

Was that the sound of a woman who was using him?

And why was it such a big deal? It was discomforting to think that that was precisely how he usually approached his relationships, although he baulked at the thought that he was *using* those women. Fair was fair: he always warned them in advance of his intentions, or rather the lack of them.

The perfect gentleman.

He didn't feel like being the perfect gentleman with Erin, and that confused him. He wanted something more…but what? Not to be written off as an amusing footnote? Was he that much of an egotist?

He wanted to shake his head clear of a murky swirl of thoughts he couldn't quite pin down and couldn't quite rationalise.

'You asked me if I'm wasting my time. Not a bit of it,' she reiterated.

'My feelings precisely.'

He skimmed her thigh with the flat of his hand and decided that there was such a thing as too much conversation.

He was a doing kind of guy. Sex was much easier. He didn't want to tackle uneasy thoughts.

Two loungers weren't ideal when it came to making love but they could have a little fun on them for a while.

He toyed with her breast, teased her nipple until it was stiff. When she began breathing quickly, he moistened his finger with his tongue and continued to play with her nipple. He was propped up on one elbow, looking at her with intense satisfaction.

Why was she so obsessed with the perfect guy? Couldn't she see that that was all just an illusion?

He cupped the mound between her thighs and then levered himself off the lounger, never removing his hand from its resting place.

Night engulfed them but a full moon threw her slender body into silvery relief.

Want slammed into him. He gently tugged her a little, urging her to slither a little lower down the lounger, legs splayed on either side so that she was open like a flower for his mouth.

He wondered, fleetingly, whether he could ever get enough of the taste of her. For a second, he just breathed her in and then darted his tongue along the slippery groove that shielded her clitoris.

He peeled the delicate folds gently apart, opening her up even more to his questing tongue, and he took his time rousing her, taking her so close to the edge and then pulling back until she began begging him to stop teasing her, whimpering that she couldn't stand it any longer, breathily panting that she needed to come.

Every uttered plea filled him with visceral pleasure. He could feel the steady pulse of his erection, demanding satisfaction.

He didn't speak as he stood up and swept her off the lounger in one smooth, hurried movement.

'You're driving me mad,' he muttered in a driven undertone. 'How do you do that to me, woman?'

He looked down at her small, perfect breasts, at the

nipples still glistening from his tongue, and wanted to come on the spot.

He made it to their cabin on the yacht in the nick of time.

The bedroom on the yacht, with its luxurious, high-end en suite, was huge. The bed was king-sized and indulgently comfortable. The air conditioning had been left on and it was cool as he nudged open the door with Erin still in his arms.

He had to clear his head to slow himself down, to make time for the little foil packet of condoms he kept by the bed.

Most of all he had to make sure not to look at her, naked and flushed on the bed. One glance at her and the unthinkable might happen.

He donned protection with shaking hands and didn't bother trying to play it cool or to take his time. He simply thrust into her, long and hard and deep on a guttural groan of fulfilment and only just managed to hold off his climax until he felt her body moving in tune with his and her orgasm tearing into her. Immediately, he came with a long shudder that left him weak in the aftermath.

He collapsed onto his back and let his breathing do its best to return to normal then he flipped onto his side and looked at her.

'You look as though you're falling asleep,' he teased. 'Is that what I do for you? Send you to sleep?'

Eyes closed, Erin smiled but then she wriggled onto her side as well and drowsily opened her eyes to look at him.

Her busy thoughts were returning.

Raffaele might enjoy this vacuum but sooner rather

than later reality was waiting for them and they would have to confront it.

When he had suggested staying on in the Caribbean, sailing down the Grenadines and taking a little time out, she had played it cool on the outside but inside, she had jumped at the idea.

He'd mentioned something about a week. He needed a break, he'd told her, holding her and kissing her, and since he was the boss he could do as he damn well pleased.

He'd grinned and told her that as his secretary, she was duty-bound to agree with him.

'We let this run its course,' he'd said with infectious confidence, 'and then we put it behind us. But if we don't see it out…it'll stay there, eating away at both of us, making it impossible to work alongside one another.'

She'd agreed.

It had sounded simple enough.

It wasn't simple now and truthfully, it never had been. She'd just kidded herself because the thought of saying goodbye to him was overwhelming.

'I guess,' she murmured without any hint of anxiety in her voice, 'we should talk about where this isn't going and start thinking about getting back to real life in London. I've been checking my emails daily and there are things waiting to be done that can't be done here, even with an internet connection.'

'Where this *isn't* going?'

'Let's not play make-believe, Raffaele,' Erin said drily. 'I know you. Don't forget I've sent many a Dear John token to girlfriends who were ushered out the back door so that you could open the front door to their replacement.'

She stroked his cheek and knew that she was mentally saying goodbye. How could she just carry on as though nothing had happened when they returned to London? He would be able to do that because he hadn't emotionally invested, but she wouldn't and that was a deep, devastating ache in her she would have to deal with over time.

She just suddenly needed to know how much time she had left with him.

'That's a little on the harsh side!'

'But untrue?'

She saw him shift uncomfortably, saw the dark flush stain his cheekbones. He couldn't deny it even if he found it a little too blunt for his liking.

'Define *untrue*.'

'You're an idiot, Raffaele.'

'I don't have a revolving door of women! And besides… you know why I never promise commitment. I've told you about my parents, their dysfunctional marriage…'

'You don't have to be afraid of committing to a relationship because the example that was set for you was a bad one.'

'No? Is that the sound of you trying to psychoanalyse me?'

'It's the sound of me trying to be logical.'

'Erin…'

'What?'

'You know who I am, don't you? You know that I'm not someone who's spent his life thinking he can't commit because he hasn't happened to find the right woman. I mean, Erin, you know that I'm not interested in commitment…'

Erin knew that this was a warning. A gentle one. This

was a fling and nothing more than that. *Don't go getting any ideas.*

'You bet. And sure, I understand that you feel you have to be careful…but will you never be tempted to settle down one day? Have a family? I don't care whether you remain a confirmed bachelor for the rest of your days. I don't care if the only companions you have when you're a wizened old man are a bunch of cats. I'm just curious.'

Raffaele couldn't help but burst out laughing. 'That's a very seductive picture you paint of me. Wizened old man? Well, if that turns out to be the case then it'll be no great shock if the only creatures that actually want to hang around me are a bunch of cats.' He paused and then said with a slight shrug. 'I expect the time will come. An heir will have to inherit the throne.' He smiled with self-irony. 'But when that time comes, I won't be doing it for love. I'll be doing it because it makes sense. No illusions that could lead to disappointment.'

'Yes, but isn't that what your parents did? Married to unite two powerful families? No illusions there that could lead to disappointment?'

'Who said either of them are disappointed?' His mouth curled derisively. 'I assume they both accepted certain terms and conditions within their union and one of those just happened to be infidelity. You'll find that there are many uber wealthy families where a lot is tolerated for the sake of the status quo.'

'But you would never tolerate that.'

'I've always been a one-woman man. That won't change if and when I ever decide to tie the knot. That said, within those parameters, I would need a woman who wasn't in search of romance, who was practical about what I could bring to the marriage. Stability, monogamy and a great deal of money. In return, I would want a calm home front, someone undemanding, there to raise whatever children we might have. Someone who would accept that I work long hours and wouldn't nag to do things I probably wouldn't have time to do.'

'Things like what?'

'Time off work for spontaneous picnics in a park somewhere…chocolate and flowers and love notes left under pillows…'

'That sounds very specific.'

Raffaele hesitated. 'I took a chance on love once upon a long time ago,' he said heavily. 'I was in my early twenties and obviously hadn't yet bought completely into the mindset I now have. Unfortunately, it didn't end well.'

'What happened?'

'She was very sweet, very wide-eyed and romantic. She was everything I wasn't and I honestly believed that if anyone could persuade me that love was possible, then it was her. I thought I could give her what she wanted but it turned out that the lessons I'd learned had been too well ingrained to be cast aside. I was building my own empire and time was in scant supply. She wanted more than the guy who worked all hours and I was puzzled by her growing demands for more of…me. When I did make an effort…she complained that I was still too wrapped up in work to give her my full attention. The sweet-natured girl turned into a shrew and I could hardly blame her.'

'How sad.'

'Timely,' Raffaele said flatly. 'We could have been

married…had kids, and then the whole situation would have been a million times more complicated. As things turned out, we ended the relationship and after a few months she actually got back in touch with me to say exactly what I felt at the time we ended things.'

'Which was?'

'That it was better the end came sooner rather than later. All's well that ended well. You'll be excited to know that she found her dream guy a year after meeting me and is now happily married with two kids. She invited me to the wedding but I thought it tactful not to go.'

Raffaele heard the cool, detached indifference in his voice when he recounted this story. Inside, though, he could feel, once again, the pain of finally accepting that that life would never be his. A life of love, vulnerability, of sharing hopes and dreams with the anchor of a woman he loved by his side.

This, what he had now, his work and his women, was his life and always would be.

And now Erin was a part of that life. He liked that. Liked the thought of them continuing what they had. And he'd figured out a way to make it possible.

Yes, it was just another relationship based on sex, but it was good, and he wasn't ready for it to be over. He'd shared a lot with her and against all odds, he had more to share. She'd got under his skin in ways he hadn't predicted and he wanted to keep her there.

His head told him *for the time being.*

His heart…? Perhaps the story was a little more nuanced. Did he dare explore those nuances?

Raffaele frowned as blurry, uneasy feelings tried to break through the logic of his thoughts.

He wouldn't allow that to happen.

'What a tender moment we're having.' He grinned, eyebrows shooting up so that she could clock the jokey sarcasm in his voice that would nullify any seriousness.

Erin looked at him in silence for a few seconds. She felt that the last of the jigsaw puzzle pieces had now been slotted into place.

Raffaele wasn't just the product of his dysfunctional family. He was also the product of a broken heart, of a relationship that had crashed and burned at that very point when hope in love had still stood a chance.

He was never going to love and as she accepted the finality of that, she realised that somewhere she had still been hoping that her impossible, ridiculous feelings would be returned.

'Yes, it's certainly very, very exciting for me to find out that the significant ex in your life is now happily married to someone else. Any more joyous anecdotes up your sleeve?' Her jokey sarcasm matched his.

Raffaele laughed under his breath. 'You have no idea how liberating it is being with a woman who has no expectations, who really and truly can live in the moment.'

Erin maintained eye contact and did something she hoped resembled an airy smile.

'We've drifted away from the topic I originally brought up,' she murmured. 'It's about time to start thinking about getting back to London. I really need to go visit my parents, make sure they're doing all right.'

'Oh yes. Not to mention those pesky emails you've checked that need urgent attention.' He grinned and smoothed her side with his hand. 'It's going to be a bit more difficult to pretend all of this never took place when we return. I thought it would be easy…a brief fling, a need sated…'

There spoke the man with the revolving-door approach to women, Erin thought sourly. However pious he might get on the subject. In Raffaele's easy-come, easy-go world, there were never any lingering after-effects once *needs were sated.*

'I've been mulling this over and hear me out because it's something I actually considered a few months ago, and this seems the perfect time to put it into practice especially since…'

'Especially since what?'

'I don't want this to end.'

Erin felt her heart skip a beat but before irrational hope could start putting feelers out, he continued, 'Not yet.' He leaned into her, kissed her, a deep, bone-meltingly thorough kiss, and at the same time he cupped her between her legs, rousing her all over again.

'And I can tell you feel the same way. Don't try to deny it. I can feel it in your wetness and I know just how turned on you'll get if I do this…'

He dipped his fingers inside her and found the beating clitoris with no trouble at all. He teased it with the expertise of a man who knew her body, knew just how to take it where it wanted to go.

Erin moaned and lost herself in sensation.

She didn't want to. There was a conversation waiting to be had but right now her body had different ideas. He moved his fingers harder and faster, and she bucked, arched and came quickly and on a long, shuddering groan of satisfaction.

'There,' he said with satisfaction. 'That's why I just can't stop this yet. Why neither of us can but…'

Erin didn't interrupt. She had no idea what he was about to say but it didn't matter because he was right. Of course they could no longer work together. Of course she would have to hand in her resignation. Even if she was greedy and decided to continue this situation, sneaking past one another during work hours and sharing hot, surreptitious glances over the computer…it would end one day and when that happened, she would be left with even more broken pieces of her heart to piece together.

He, on the other hand, would always escape unscathed because he would never be emotionally invested.

'Want to hear my plan? I think you'll love it, Erin, and honestly, it's something I should have done, like I said, some time ago.'

'Okay. What's your plan? Tell me. I'm all ears.'

'I promote you. You earned a promotion a long time ago and I'm not talking a salary increase. I'm talking about a complete change of job title.'

He paused and in that pause Erin understood. She saw it all in an instant, how he'd worked things out.

The details, the job title, they weren't important: what it boiled down to was that Raffaele planned to pay her to continue their affair. Although she had no doubt that he would never see it that way.

'Really?' she said, trying to keep her devastation out of her voice.

'I want you to take full charge of a number of clients, including this chain of hotels if I go ahead with the purchase, which I probably will. Your clients will all be familiar to you and you'll have full responsibility to see the ongoing projects through to their conclusion. Naturally, with the title will come a substantial pay increase. Erin, you'll be able to afford to move out from that peculiar place you live in, to give your parents whatever financial help they need…to lead a life of comfort doing the thing you love.'

'Oh wow.' She wasn't tempted for a second. Money could never buy what she really wanted.

'I know! You'll be reporting to me, Erin, but you'll be on a different floor completely so there will be no awkwardness.'

'I see.' Conveniently relocated—near enough to be accessible for as long as it took before he got bored but far enough so that he didn't have to face her on a daily basis once the whole thing had ground to a halt.

'I've started the ball rolling with HR,' he told her comfortably. 'I hope you don't mind? So here's what I'm thinking…a couple more days here and then back to the grindstone except…the grindstone isn't going to be quite what either of us left behind. No…it's going to be a lot more exciting now… You can take a week or so off, go visit your parents, and by the time you return to the office, you'll be the proud possessor of a shiny new desk in a shiny new office on the fourth floor.'

'That's all very speedy, Raffaele.'

'I like to think of myself as a man of action.'

'I see.'

'Am I detecting a certain lack of enthusiasm?' Raffaele frowned and drew back to look at her. 'Aren't you excited? Don't you *want* what's on the table?' His voice roughened with sincerity. 'You get the job of a lifetime,

Erin, and we get to keep this going, to sleep together, to touch one another…'

There was just the briefest of hesitations. Erin looked down then back to him. She smiled.

'Keep it going,' she murmured. 'Yes…we both still want one another…so why not keep it going?'

For precisely the length of time they remained on this yacht. Why not indeed? A couple of days of being greedy, of having Raffaele all to herself. And then the minute they returned to London…the only thing on the table would be her resignation.

CHAPTER NINE

ERIN WAS TEMPTED to email her resignation letter. So much easier. Something brief and anodyne with a few vague words about the many challenges the job had given her but alas…circumstances dictated that she now seek alternative employment. Something high on waffle and low on detail.

Then she would cite holiday time still owing, which would allow her to resign without having to set foot in the office again.

In the end she decided to hand the letter to Raffaele herself and deal with the consequences head-on.

How bad could it be anyway? As far as she knew there were no dungeons in the building into which she could be flung because his offer had been rejected. She expected he would be startled but then he would shrug and accept the inevitable.

She'd never known Raffaele to beg for anything in all the time she'd been working for him. When it came to women, he was good at walking away. His nose might be put out of joint because the walking-away schedule had not been set by him, but habit would kick in and the only thing he would really miss would be her efficiency in the office.

She was a bundle of nerves on the Monday morning as she strode into the lift and headed up to the top floor.

Cruising down the Grenadines felt like a lifetime ago even though they'd only returned two days previously, from the sticky humidity to the uncomfortable heat of the city.

Her resignation letter was burning a hole in her bag.

How was it that everything around her was so familiar, from the people greeting her to the buzz of employees ditching their jackets and settling down for a day's work, and yet she felt as though she was having an out-of-body experience?

Raffaele was, of course, already in. There was something about the atmosphere on the floor when he was in, a certain alertness, a tacit awareness that the big guy was around, which meant everyone went into hyper-focus mode.

She waved and nodded to people she knew as she walked towards the office she and Raffaele shared. It was at the very end of a corridor that housed the various directors behind smoked-glass walls.

She breathed in to steady her nerves, pushed open the door and then walked straight through the connecting door. Raffaele was on the phone, his seat pushed back from his desk.

He came off his call with alacrity and looked at her with intense satisfaction before vaulting to his feet to perch on his desk, the very picture of an alpha male in possession of just what he happened to want.

'I thought you were taking some time out to go visit your parents. How are they, by the way? Told them about us yet?' He grinned and moved to shut the connecting door, locking them into his office space.

'I decided that my time might be better served coming in to work today.'

'Got it. Fully on board with that one.' He reached to sift his fingers through her hair. 'The sun loves you. You're an incredible golden colour after a couple of weeks in it. Brings out your freckles.' He deposited a kiss lightly on her lips and for a couple of seconds, Erin's world stopped and she was besieged by memories of how her body felt whenever he touched it.

As though he could literally control her ability to think or not think.

Right now, he barrelled straight through her defences and she felt herself go weak at the knees.

She put her hand on his chest, felt the beating of his heart underneath the white shirt and pushed him away although it was a very wobbly, unconvincing push.

'I know,' he breathed, not budging. 'I get it. Very reckless of us to carry on within the confines of the office. Much better for us to meet outside. Office gossip can spread faster than a flu virus, but which of us would be able to resist if we happened to be within ten metres of one another? Hence why working on a different floor might help our blood pressure.' He slanted a wicked smile. 'But I get why you had to come in. Believe me, I'm on the same page. The thought of not being able to touch you for another fortnight was bringing me out in a cold sweat. I realise I might not be a fan of delayed gratification after all. I might have had to spring a surprise visit on your parents.'

Erin was temporarily distracted by that appalling thought.

She wriggled away from him and moved to her usual chair in front of his desk in a pointed attempt to put some distance between them. Not much but any small amount of distance would do.

He, in turn, returned to perch on the desk, which left her with the heart-stopping sight of his muscular thighs and the fabric of his trousers pulled tight across them. She stared, dry mouthed for few seconds, at his hands hanging loosely between his knees and cleared her throat.

'That would have been a terrible idea,' she croaked distractedly.

'Under normal circumstances, yes,' Raffaele agreed. He didn't take his eyes off her for a single second. 'Under normal circumstances, the last thing I've ever been interested in is getting to know the parents. But then your parents are in a league of their own.'

'Am I supposed to take that as a compliment?'

'Insofar as that would be a first for me,' he murmured without skipping a beat. 'But then, in so many ways, you're a first for me.'

'I'm duly flattered,' Erin said politely. She wasn't. Being seen as a novelty was no great compliment and that was what it came down to, wasn't it? Plus, did he really think that seeing her parents as oddballs in 'a league of their own' was going to have her heart racing? That she was going to be bowled over by the fact that he might want to meet them the way a scientist might be interested in meeting someone from another planet?

Erin knew that she was being unfair.

Raffaele was a naturally curious person and he was

genuinely curious about her parents. In a lot of ways she couldn't blame him. They couldn't have been further removed from his own stuffy, cold family, the people too rooted in tradition to give their only child the basic love and affection he had once craved.

No amount of money could buy love and affection.

'So how are we going to play this?' Raffaele murmured silkily. 'Heads down until five thirty and then we go our separate ways and meet up at an agreed time at my place?'

'Since when have you ever left this office at five thirty?'

'Since when have I ever had an irresistible and compelling reason to?'

'Wait, is that another compliment, Raffaele?'

'Now that you mention it, I do believe it is. I'm very tempted to lock the outside door and make love to you right now on my desk.'

'Raffaele…' She drew in a deep, steadying breath and edged her chair a couple of inches back. 'I'm not actually here because I couldn't bear the thought of being apart from you for a week and a half.'

'No?' But his smile told her that he wasn't fully convinced.

She rummaged in her bag and pulled out the envelope.

'What's that?' He frowned but didn't actually take it from her.

'An old-fashioned method of communication,' she said, buying time. 'Only just a little more advanced than carrier pigeon.' She cleared her throat and stared at the envelope. 'Raffaele, it's my letter of resignation.'

The silence settled between them like lead. She

watched his expression turn from amusement to disbelief to shock.

Erin had known what lay ahead and she had made sure to enjoy every second of the time she had left with him. Their love-making had been intense…hot…incomparable. Once or twice, in the throes of passion, she had come so close to telling him how she felt about him but she had held her tongue.

Her dignity was important to her. She had already revealed so much of herself to him but that last secret would be hers to hold close to her chest forever.

'Are you going to take it?' she asked.

'No.'

'What do you mean *no*?'

'You're not going to resign. I can scarcely believe I'm hearing this at all!'

He leapt to his feet and strode to the huge bank of floor-to-ceiling windows that dominated his massive office. For a few seconds she stared through him, his body taut with tension, then he spun around and looked at her narrowly.

'What's happened?' he demanded. 'What's changed? No, don't tell me. You've told your parents everything and they insisted that you keep your distance. Is that it?'

'I'm not following you, Raffaele.'

'It's easy enough!' He raked his fingers through his hair and smiled grimly. 'Your parents want the best for you. You've told me often enough how attached you are to them, how anxious they were when you broke up with that creep years ago. I expect you told them that you were involved with someone who wasn't into walking up the aisle anytime soon and they promptly told you that the best thing you could do would be to walk away. Did you tell them about the deal we had? The promotion? Did you mention the fun we have together? *Did you bother to make the point that having fun is a pretty damn important part of being alive?*'

'Raffaele…'

'Let me meet them. I'll talk to them. I'll convince them that what we have is good for you!'

Was that desperation Raffaele heard in his own voice? Was this him? Were these his insides tearing to shreds at the thought that she was leaving him?

The last thing he'd expected was for Erin to walk away. After his generous offer, after the promotion of a lifetime, after establishing that they still wanted one another.

Especially after those last few days they'd spent together.

Magical.

Just when, hell, he'd begun to see those nuances… begun to feel things he'd never thought he was capable of feeling.

No! The thought of his own weakness was enough to have him balling his hands into impotent fists. He *refused* to lose control, *to lose perspective.*

'No! Raffaele, I haven't told my parents about us although I'm pretty sure you're right. I'm pretty sure they'd be horrified. I'm leaving because what we had was great and it was fun but I want to move on with my life and that life doesn't have you in it. If I stay here, having this fling with you, I'm going to soon start thinking that I'm wasting my time.'

'Wasting your time?'

'Don't sound so horrified. Although I'm guessing this is the first time any woman has said something like that to you.'

'How can having fun be *wasting time*?'

'I suppose,' Erin said thoughtfully, 'I was in a deep freeze when it came to men…and then this thing happened between us. And it was terrific and I had a lot of fun but I realised that to come back here, to return to reality, and then to just awkwardly carry on having fun that was going nowhere would be doing myself a disservice.'

The ground under Raffaele's feet, that rock-solid confidence in himself and his impregnability when it came to his emotions, was shifting.

He refused to let go of the philosophy of total independence that had ruled his life for so long. *Absolutely refused.* But inside, his heart was no longer playing ball with his head. 'You're saying you want some kind of a long-term relationship with me? A ring on your finger? Marriage and two-point-two kids?'

'No!'

Yes!

Raffaele didn't know how close he'd got to the truth, that Erin couldn't be with him because he wasn't into commitment. He just thought that her parents were to blame. In reality, Erin secretly suspected that they might be happy for her to be having fun…might actually agree with Raffaele if he showed up on their doorstep bringing tales of adventure and excitement.

What would he do if she were to tell him the truth? That *she* was the one who wanted too much, that she'd had her fun and now it was time to move on because here, back in the real world, those snatched moments of joy would quickly become a growing groundswell of the pain of unrequited love.

They stared at one another in momentary silence.

'In short, you believe you deserve better than me,' Raffaele said heavily.

Erin's heart constricted. She gazed at his downturned mouth, the lowered eyes fringed by those thick sooty lashes, eyes that were so good at concealing what he didn't want the world to know.

That there was a well of emotional insecurity inside him, the legacy of cold, distant parents who might not have been cruel but had been emotionally neglectful. The boy whose heart had sealed up had become the young man whose one attempt at love had failed. Now here he was before her...the adult who had locked his heart away for good because the lessons he'd learned had been just too hard.

He was right.

She did deserve better. She deserved to love a guy who could actually return her feelings. When she tried to picture this mythical creature, her mind went blank.

'I know what I want,' she said, tilting her chin, voice firm, 'and yes, it's someone who really does want the whole deal and that's what I intend to do now. Dave was a creep and for a while I decided to think that all men were creeps. It was easy and lazy to take a step back from dating, in case I just so happened to run into another man like that—I know that now. But those days are gone, thanks to you.'

'Good to hear I've been useful.'

Erin heard the cynical edge to his voice and could already sense the distance he was putting between them. Pride was slamming into place and his desire to find an explanation for the inexplicable was being ruthlessly stamped out.

'I have some holiday saved,' she said, 'quite a bit, as a matter of fact. Of course, if you want me to train my replacement up, then I'm happy to oblige but—'

'I think I can handle that myself.'

He moved back to his leather chair behind the desk, establishing the boundaries between them, returning to his role of boss and relegating her once again to her role as his secretary. Putting a full stop to anything else that had existed between them.

'I'll spend the day making notes on the accounts for whoever replaces me…contact names and so on…'

'Whoever replaces you will survive fine without notes.'

Raffaele was still reeling. Through his shock and angry bewilderment, he was already being forced to acknowledge just how deeply Erin had burrowed inside him. He didn't know what to do with the tumult of raw emotions brought to the surface by her casual dismissal of him as a guy she'd just *had a little fun with*.

He'd seen her walk through that door unexpectedly and his heart had lifted. He hadn't been able to stop thinking about her, projecting to when she'd be back to take up her new role…and to pick up where they'd left off.

When she had appeared in the doorway to his office,

he'd felt a wave of intense satisfaction that she was on the same page as him.

That surge of pleasure felt like a lifetime ago now.

He couldn't believe that he'd patted himself on the back at the arrangement that was now in place, one in which they could carry on seeing one another, sating this weird, powerful need that was driving them both, without the awkwardness of being within the same four walls.

And it wasn't as if he had created a superfluous role to accommodate their affair! He'd simply done what he'd been thinking of doing for a while, promoting her to the level of her potential.

All around could there have been a more satisfying conclusion? No.

He'd been so pleased with himself. He'd enjoyed imagining her happiness at what lay ahead of them. Not just a continuation of this compelling, addictive relationship but a promotion for her that would come with a hefty salary increase, more than enough for her vacate her sad rented accommodation and to think about buying somewhere without sacrificing the financial help she was committed to giving her parents.

But now…

How wrong he'd been about everything. For the first time in his memory, he'd had the rug pulled from under his feet and he didn't know what to do about it.

The one thing he wasn't going to do was beg. He would deal with whatever was going on inside him later, in solitude. He had access to huge resources of inner strength. He would call upon them in due course to combat the tsunami of frenzied, inexplicable, tumultuous emotion rushing through him.

'When?' he asked in a roughened undertone, as she remained hovering indecisively in front of him.

She'd effectively dumped him. No fuss, no warning. So why was he bothering to prolong the conversation?

Because he cared. Jesus, how and when had that happened? How and when had he *allowed* that to happen?

'When what?'

'When did you decide that the deal on the table wasn't going to do?' He scowled at his own weakness.

Erin sighed and reddened.

Was this going as expected? Sure, she'd known that his pride would be hurt but she'd figured that he'd recover fast and shrug it all off.

She *had* expected him to try to talk her into staying. That was why she'd had the *holiday time left outstanding* on the tip of her tongue, as a way to wriggle out of spending more time in his company, which would have meant more time absorbing him, breathing him in, falling harder and deeper in love.

It stung to realise just how disposable he thought she was.

Her defence mechanisms swung into place and she looked at him coolly and distantly.

'When you made that offer… I knew that I wasn't going to take you up on it.'

'Right.'

'I guess it put things into sharp focus.' *One hundred percent true.*

'Understood.'

'There was also a part of me that felt…as though you

were paying me, somehow, to continue with what we had because you weren't quite ready to end it.'

'Paying you?'

'You can hardly blame me for thinking that.' But her colour mounted at the outrage in his voice and it made her feel small that she had even harboured that treacherous thought, even though *it made perfect sense.*

Although, she now thought, didn't it make just as much sense that she might have *wanted* to see the worst in him? Because doing that gave her the courage to walk away?

'I told you that was something that was already on the cards. It was a well-deserved promotion. When have I ever lied to you?'

'You haven't but—'

'But you decided that it would be a good idea to turn me into the bad guy? I thought you knew me better than that, Erin.'

'Raffaele…'

He waved his hand in a dismissive gesture but for a few seconds, she remained where she was, dithering, filled with a sickening sense of deep loss.

It was devastating for her to think that she would leave this man forever and with the impression that, for all that he'd told her about himself—and it was probably more than he realised—she'd never really known him at all.

He shrugged, his face cool and remote and striking at the very core of her.

'One last thing,' he said, 'and this from the guy you thought had fabricated a job opportunity as some kind of coercive piece of bribery…'

'Raffaele, please…don't. I…'

'You won't see me again. We're done and dusted. But the job is still yours for the taking.'

'What do you mean?'

'I mean the job I offered you…still stands and it has nothing to do with whether we were lovers once or not. It stands because you would be good at it and you deserve it.' He stood up, bringing the conversation to a close. 'You can think about it and let Human Resources know if you're still interested. If not, you can rest assured that the reference you get from me will be of the highest order.'

'Thank you,' Erin whispered, tears stinging the back of her eyes. She spun around before they could start streaming down. When she looked over her shoulder, one last, quick glance, it was to see him binning the envelope with her resignation letter inside. He hadn't even bothered to read it.

Raffaele heard the sound of her shuffling in her office, clearing her stuff out. He could picture her so clearly, could see the soft curve of her neck, the slenderness of her arms, the delicate bone structure of her face with those freckles that had appeared from nowhere in the heat of the sun.

He slammed his fist on his desk, strode restlessly to the window and looked down at the streets below. From here, he had a bird's-eye view of the people entering and leaving the building. He felt nailed to the spot.

Erin had left her office. He'd heard the quiet click of the outer door closing. He wondered whether she would say anything to any of her colleagues, or whether she would just disappear into a future that no longer included him or anyone else she had spent the past four years working with.

His heart *hurt*. He only had himself to blame. That was what came from being foolish enough to lower your guard.

He remained where he was, looking down, waiting to see her hurrying out and away from his orbit.

He wanted to tear himself away, return to the pile of emails waiting for him, but he realised that ever since this three-dimensional, fascinating, sexy, addictive woman had entered his life, work had taken a back seat.

But what would staring through a window do for him? Except ratchet up his levels of frustration? Frustration and basic incomprehension. He had made her an irresistible offer. They still wanted one another. To him, her reasoning for walking away, for *dumping him because he'd served his purpose*, made no sense.

But then again…

Raffaele frowned and thought about them both, thought about his own life experiences and about hers.

His formative years, spent cocooned in wealth but lacking the joy of loving, demonstrative parents, had toughened him and his doomed love affair had snuffed out any last remaining dregs of hope that love was for him.

He realised with a jolt how little real interest he had ever taken in the backstories of the women he had dated in the past. He had entered all those relationships with his emotions sealed off and, unable to share anything of himself, had never sought to discover anything about his partners.

He wined and dined them and pleasured them and then when it was over, he walked away intact.

But he had found out about Erin. He had begun to feel…things stirring inside him, like small shoots wanting to grow.

But as she had made perfectly clear, he'd never been her type.

She was someone whose entire background had geared her towards the eventual goal of a long-term relationship. Where he was content to have fun until the fun ended, she wasn't. Their intense physical connection had made her realise that she wanted more. Who could blame her? He was cut from completely different cloth.

She did deserve better than him.

All told, it was a good thing that she had broken things off. However disoriented he felt at the moment, he would and could never be the straightforward kind of guy who wanted the neat house and the picket fence and the apple tree in the back garden.

Raffaele stared sightlessly down for a few seconds.

His heart picked up pace.

Yet what might it feel like to have had her love? To have seen that soft smile turn to him with tenderness as well as passion? To see love in her eyes as well as desire? To know that she had his back?

He gritted his teeth in frustration. He'd tried all that in the past and it hadn't worked. He didn't have it in him to return that depth of feeling. He was too conditioned by his past, however weirdly she'd made him feel.

About to swing away from the window, something caught his eye. The navy blue outfit, so severe considering it was summer. The glossy chestnut hair tied back in her attempt to look professional. How could she not know that when he saw that, he also saw it loose and tumbling as she moved beneath him, flushed with lust?

Erin…and next to her…

Raffaele squinted, his entire body stilling at the figure by her side and then freezing as she fell against the man standing in front of her and was enveloped in an embrace that brought a surge of primitive jealousy exploding in his veins.

He spun away and walked to his desk and sat down, everything inside him in turmoil as he replayed in his head what he had just seen.

Best forgotten, he told himself fiercely.

She'd made her choice and he would never beg for anyone.

'I'm so sorry,' Erin pulled back from Colin, shocked at how easily she had blurted everything out to him.

She'd been hurrying out of the offices with her few possessions in a carrier bag and there he was, coming in as she was going out, and the second he had seen her white face he had pulled her to one side and asked her if she was okay.

And the floodgates had opened. A few concerned words from a guy she barely knew and she had burst into tears.

'This isn't me,' she sniffed, rummaging in her bag for the packet of tissues she always kept there. 'I don't blab and I don't… I don't blub either. And I really, *really* don't share the sort of stuff I've just shared with you. I… Please, you must promise me that you won't say a word.'

'Of course I won't. You forget I'm a lawyer. Lawyers are very good at keeping their own counsel. I kind of knew something was up between the two of you,' he said thoughtfully. 'Not sure how but it was a feeling I got when I glanced over at one point at that party at his house and saw the body language between you. Erin, want to go somewhere and talk?'

'I... No... I should go back home. I need some time on my own.'

'Sure?'

'You're very kind, Colin.' She struggled with a smile and he laughed ruefully.

'I'm not convinced that that's such a great thing to be. What do they say about nice guys finishing last?'

'There's everything right with being a nice guy. You're just the sort of man I should be looking for.' Erin was oddly comfortable saying that.

'But sometimes life doesn't work out that way.'

'No.'

'Will you do me the enormous favour of keeping in touch?'

'Of course I will. I've made loads of good friends here and as soon as I've got my act together, I'll be in touch with all of them.' She sighed. 'In the meanwhile, I shall take a little time out of London.'

'Erin...this probably won't do you much good but... he's a guy who breaks hearts.'

'I know. Don't worry. This heart will mend.'

But would it? And if it ever did, how long would it take?

She was mentally and physically exhausted by the end of the evening. It had been a long day. Life had changed irrevocably in a matter of hours and even though she'd thought she'd braced herself for it, even though she'd spent those last few days on that yacht *knowing* that she would be handing in her resignation as soon as they returned to London, she *still* found that she was unprepared for the enormity of the decision.

Should she have accepted Raffaele's offer? Would another month or so made such a difference? Would her heart have hurt any the less?

He had offered her riches beyond her wildest dreams. A promotion that would have taken her physically out of his orbit, so that she wouldn't have had to see him on a day-to-day basis. She could have carried on there once their *situation* had come to an end, continued with a high-flying career that would have sorted all her financial problems and given her the sort of job satisfaction she could never have found anywhere else.

Had she been *stupid* not to have bitten his hand off for that job promotion?

But no.

A clean break was what was necessary. Anything else would have been the equivalent of the alcoholic thinking that just one drink a day would be okay.

The shock to her system would fade but if she'd chosen to stay, bumping into him now and again…seeing some woman click-clack her way up to his office in passing… Well, she would have lived in a state of semi-permanent misery.

A little break would do her good and when she returned to London, it would be time to start hunting down another job and getting back to the dating scene!

It sounded good, she tried to tell herself. She couldn't wait.

It was after ten in the evening, when being alone with

her thoughts was driving her crazy, that she phoned her parents.

'Hi, Mum?'

'What's wrong, Erin?'

Erin's voice wobbled. 'I'm coming home.' She looked around her, looked at her rented place with its dreary four walls, as unlived in as if she'd only moved there an hour ago. 'And I might just be staying for good…'

CHAPTER TEN

ONE WEEK.

One week of torture. Raffaele hadn't been able to sleep. Worse, he hadn't been able to work. He'd cancelled meetings. Had delegated the search for Erin's replacement to one of the PAs who worked for his finance director and was indifferent to whatever qualifications they came with.

'Just as long as they're competent, can tell the difference between a computer and a microwave and over forty-five.' Man or woman, he didn't care.

He stared, scowling at his office door, which was shut. The adjoining office where Erin used to sit was empty. He could still remember the soft sound of her packing her stuff and the gentle click of the outer door as she'd let herself out of the office and out of his life for good.

He pushed himself away from his desk and swivelled the chair so that he was staring out of the window then clasped his hands behind his head and succumbed to yet another pointless bout of thinking.

How much thinking could one guy do? Shouldn't thoughts run out sooner or later?

For the millionth time he thought of Colin, the guy who'd been flirting with Erin at the party he'd thrown a few weeks back. Mr Dependable Lawyer, who was probably just the sort of solid, reliable man Erin should go for.

Not him. Not Raffaele Rossi, the guy with the broken background who had only ever reliably lived up the dubious role of heartbreaker.

He was the last man she should go for, which was why he'd been good for a bit of fun but nothing more.

Had he wanted more than that? From her?

The question, which had been plaguing him for the past week, inserted itself into his consciousness once again, and Raffaele leaned back against the chair and sighed.

He knew that answer to that. Why bother fighting it? He'd tried. He really had. She'd walked out on him and he'd immediately told himself that it was for the best. He'd seen her with Colin and also immediately told himself that that also was for the best.

Women came and went and if she'd left a hole in his life then it was because she had been the one to leave prematurely, because she'd worked for him, because their arrangement hadn't been the usual one he was accustomed to.

Blah, blah, blah.

Underneath all of that, the feelings unleashed in him had refused to go away and hadn't paid a scrap of attention to the voice of reason.

He'd opened up his heart to Erin and he couldn't seem to escape the consequences of that.

Each line of thought he'd taken to try to avoid that fact had crashed into a brick wall, a dead end. Now Raffaele, in the quiet of his office at one forty-five on a Tuesday afternoon, finally accepted what he'd been dodging for the past week.

Longer.

He'd fallen in love with her. And what he'd wanted in return hadn't been *fun.* What he'd wanted in return had been her love.

And now another man was on the scene.

Some guy she deserved. Who deserved her.

Raffaele banged his fist on his desk and shot up to his feet. He didn't give a damn who deserved who, and he was done with this game of pretending that everything was just fine and that all he wanted was the best for her. Yes, he damn well wanted the best for her! Just so long as it included *him*…

Step one…he'd find Colin, do his best to keep calm and find out what she was up to, whether there was something there, some budding relationship. If there was? Well, that would change nothing. He needed to see Erin, needed to tell her how he felt, and no one was going to stand in his way.

Erin was watching telly when the doorbell went.

Her parents were out and she was guiltily pleased about that.

'You deserve to have a bit of time out,' she had urged them both the evening before. 'Dad, I know you think you have to be careful with money all of the time but you don't. Having dinner out now and again is a good thing. It's not extravagant. Not unless you go to that place by the town hall where you have to remortgage your house to afford a starter.' She'd laughed. They'd laughed. But it had still taken a lot of persuasion to get them to make a booking somewhere and to propel them through the front door an hour ago.

They were both so grateful to her for her financial input even though she told them that there was no need. They were also so concerned about her, about her break-up, about her career now that she had fled London with no plans to return unless it proved impossible to get work locally… The weight of their anxiety was wearying. Now, with them both out of the house, for the first time in a week Erin felt that she could actually stop pretending to be okay. She could stop smiling till her jaw ached.

She could relax as much as it was possible to react when the only thing on her mind was Raffaele. He occupied so much of her thoughts that she had occasional moments of despair, when she wondered whether she would ever be able to clear her head of him.

The memory of clearing out her office, gathering up the few personal bits and pieces and stuffing them into a carrier bag, was as vivid as if it had happened minutes ago.

She'd stood outside, talking to Colin, unwilling in some weird way to break the connection with the place she had worked for such a long time, with the man to whom she had lost her heart. She had felt scared and overwhelmed and adrift. But then Colin had finally and reluctantly left, and she'd taken one last look up to the bank of glass through which she had peered through countless times, hoping for a final glimpse of Raffaele. But of course he wasn't there, staring out like some lovelorn teenager.

He'd was already behind his computer, already putting her to the back of his mind the way he'd done with all those other women he'd dated in the past once their time with him had come to an end.

The sound of the doorbell ringing again, this time more insistently, finally cut through her memories and she reluctantly stood up.

It was a little after seven thirty in the evening, the sun was shining outside and it was still warm enough to be sitting out in the back garden. She felt lazy and slothful cooped up inside wearing some faded cotton trousers with ridiculous cartoon characters all over them and an old T-shirt she had found in one of the drawers in the bedroom she used whenever she came down to see her parents.

She didn't want to answer the door. She didn't want to speak to anyone. She wanted to wallow in dismal thoughts and then lose herself in whatever terrible television show she could locate on the few channels her parents had on their telly.

She was ready with her excuses when she pulled open the door to find…the very man she'd been thinking about standing on the doorstep.

Or was it?

Was she hallucinating? Had her fevered thoughts conjured up the one person in the world who was occupying all the space in her head?

'Erin.'

'Raffaele? What are you doing here?'

'Will you let me in?'

'How did you find out where I was? How did you get hold of my parents' address?'

'I asked the lawyer. Told him I had some confidential

papers to give you and I wanted to deliver them personally in case you had any questions.'

'Who are you talking about? What lawyer?'

'The one who was chatting you up at my party.'

'The lawyer has a name and you still haven't told me what you're doing here. You can't just *show up on my parents' doorstep* without warning.'

'I thought that if I warned you I was coming, you might have not wanted to see me.'

'Why?'

Belatedly, Erin remembered that he knew nothing of her broken heart, nothing of her feelings for him. To Raffaele, everything was as it should be and if he was standing on her doorstep now then it was because there was some work-related issue he wanted to discuss.

Or maybe he wanted to plead with her to fall back into bed with him. He could be a dog with a bone if he wanted something that wasn't going his way.

For a few treacherous seconds, Erin played with that tantalising thought before reluctantly boxing it up and shoving it to the side.

'Why wouldn't I want to see you, Raffaele?'

Raffaele's mouth had been dry ever since he'd seen her standing there in the doorway. She was wearing some pyjama bottoms with gaudy cartoon figures splashed over them and a T-shirt that had Bargain Basement stamped all over it and he had never seen anything sexier in his life before.

'Because of the way things ended between us. Felt like we parted on a regrettably sour note. Look, let me in. Are your parents here? I won't be long. You have my word.'

Erin shifted and Raffaele stepped into the small, attractive house and had a quick look around him.

It was quiet here. The cottage was at the end of a peaceful lane and was surrounded by hedgerows and low stone walls. Inside there were beams and whitewashed walls and clutter.

Lots of clutter. A pile of books stacked by the side of the front door, pictures on the walls and lots of them, all framed family photos. Through the open door he could see the sitting room with squashy sofas and a rug and yet more framed family photos and in the background he could hear the sound of the television.

He liked open space, clean lines and absolutely no clutter whatsoever. He should have hated this, but he immediately felt at home.

'Things ended fine between us,' Erin quickly contradicted. 'I told you I wasn't prepared to carry on sleeping with you until the whole thing fizzled out and then I packed my stuff and left.'

'Afterwards I wondered whether you might have been offended because I offered you that promotion.'

'Why would I have been offended? It was a very generous offer.'

'Could we sit? Maybe I could have something to drink. I've spent quite some time on the road.'

Erin sighed.

She didn't want him here and yet she felt as though she'd never wanted anything more in her life. She didn't want to look at him but her rebellious eyes couldn't help but stray, and oh, how beautiful he was. He was an assault on the senses and she could feel herself spinning back to square one. The pain of not having him in her life was hitting her all over again, full force.

Maybe he'd come to check in on her.

He was naturally intuitive and yes, he might have sensed that after their amazing time together, there had been something cool and remote when she had said goodbye. Maybe her unhappiness had somehow got through to him and, as the friend he had always been, he'd felt compelled to come and find out what was going on.

But with the parameters altered between them, he'd felt awkward about announcing his intention.

She didn't care, and she hated herself for second-guessing.

'Colin should never have told you where I was staying. It was out of order for him to give you my address.'

She walked towards the kitchen, keenly aware of Raffaele just behind her. Every nerve in her body was alert to his towering presence behind her.

'I can make you a coffee and you can tell me why you're here and then you can head back to London, Raffaele. Or else there's a hotel in the village if you'd rather check in there and save yourself the trip back. My parents are out at the moment and I'd rather you weren't around when they get back.'

'Why?'

'Why what?' Stretching up to reach a mug from the cupboard, Erin spun around and looked at him with undisguised hostility. She didn't care what he read into her expression.

In a rush, she felt a tidal wave of resentment that he had shown up here, in the very place in which she had come to take refuge. She needed to get him out of her system but right now, with him crowding her in the small, cosy kitchen, every inch of her system was lit up by him.

'Look, Raffaele, if you've come to discuss some stupid work thing, then there was no need to trek all the way down here to sort it out. I did offer to stay and do a handover if that was what you wanted, but you refused.'

'I know. I'm not here about some stupid work thing, Erin. Come. Sit. Forget the coffee. I'll survive without it. Please.'

Erin hesitated. He looked exhausted. Haggard. She hadn't really noticed before because she'd been too wrapped up with dealing with her own emotions.

'I've been a fool' was the first thing he said when she was seated on the chair at the pine kitchen table, facing him.

His hands were resting loosely on the table and he had spoken so softly that she'd had to strain to hear what he was saying.

'What are you talking about?'

'I let you go.'

Raffaele looked at her and as their eyes tangled, he realised that he'd never felt more vulnerable.

He also realised that this wasn't the first time he'd felt this way. She'd unlocked a piece of him a long time ago. He just hadn't realised it until they'd become lovers. Then all those things he'd shared with her had, piece by piece, unlocked more and more of his frozen heart.

But still he'd refused point blank to admit it.

'You didn't *let me go*, Raffaele,' Erin said, sounding confused. 'I decided that I couldn't carry on working for you because I would have found it too awkward even if we weren't physically sharing the same space, and because I felt it was a good time to branch out. So…'

'I've never shared myself with anyone the way I shared myself with you.'

'You've had a million lovers.'

'A million might be just a tiny bit of an exaggeration.' But he half smiled and held her gaze without flinching. 'Erin, I never shared any of myself with any of them. I took them out, wined and dined them, had fun with them but they remained strangers, even if they didn't take a similar view. With you…? I think I've been sharing bits of myself for years without paying the slightest bit of attention to it. And then when we became lovers… I foolishly assumed that I was going to remain immune to any woman having influence over my emotions.'

'You're saying…' Erin whispered. 'I don't get what you're saying.'

'I'm saying that I fell in love with you, Erin. I never saw it coming but then, when I think about it, it came in small steps and all those small steps were invisible at the time.'

'Fell in love…?'

'I had so many opportunities to tell you. When you said that you were leaving, when you handed me that resignation letter, the bottom of my world dropped out. But even then I was in denial, too afraid to admit that I'd given my heart and soul to someone, that I had relinquished power over my own feelings and emotions, which was something I swore I'd never do.'

'I just can't believe that you're saying all this, Raffaele.'

'I know. I also know that I took a chance coming

here. When I saw you standing outside the office with the lawyer—'

'You *saw* me…? With Colin? But when? I haven't been back to London since coming down here.'

'On the day you left,' Raffaele said, flushing. He'd never felt more exposed but now he'd started, there were no signposts showing him how to veer off down another road, not that he wanted to. No, he wanted to share all of himself with the woman sitting opposite him, revealing nothing but on the other hand not turfing him out.

It gave him a glimmer of hope.

And then hope took wing and really began to soar when she reached forward and covered his hand with hers, then linked their fingers together.

He held those fingers tight, never wanting to let go.

'I was jealous as hell of the man,' he admitted gruffly. 'And I was jealous of him at the party as well, even though I swept that aside, barely acknowledged it. It took everything inside me to be civil when I went to ask him about your whereabouts. It even occurred to me that I could have him transferred to another office—New York appealed—so that he was no longer competition on my doorstep.'

Erin smiled.

She squeezed his hand. If she could have bottled this moment forever, she would have.

'You have no idea how tough the past week's been for me,' she confessed, her voice low, her heart beating fast as she strove to match his honesty with her own.

She'd spent so many years holding on to what she'd thought was a harmless crush, only for it to blossom into something far more dangerous to her peace of mind. Now she felt as though her emotions were waiting impatiently to burst their banks.

'Tell me,' Raffaele urged.

'You've been honest with me so I'm going to be completely honest with you,' Erin confided huskily. 'I've had a crush on you for years.' She reddened at the confession. She half turned away from his reaction but after just a second of surprise, his face registered satisfaction that thrilled her to the core and gave her the confidence to continue.

'Tell me more. I'm all ears.'

'That's more like it.' Erin grinned and then leaned forward to kiss him delicately on the side of his mouth only to succumb to something deeper and hungrier and more demanding when he cradled the back of her neck and properly returned her kiss.

'What do you mean?' he murmured, drawing back but keeping his hand on her neck, holding her close.

'The brimming-over-with-self-confidence guy I ended up finding irresistible.'

'Nope. Don't recognise myself in that description.' He kissed her again, a lingering kiss that left her trembling for more. 'Although I'm very much liking the finding-irresistible part of what you just said. I think we should explore that line in a little more depth.'

'You're so full of yourself.'

'And yet you fell in love with me…'

'Yes, I did. I just thought that it was a harmless crush, a reaction to a broken heart, a safe refuge until I got my act together and started dating again. But the weeks became months and I guess I should have stopped and asked myself why I was stuck in a routine of fantasising about you instead of getting on with finding a guy…'

'It's so easy to work things out in retrospect. I could say the same about myself, about the way I found myself confiding in you without wondering how it was that something I loathed doing with other women came so easy to me when I was doing it to you. Signposts ignored.'

'Yes.' Erin nodded. 'And then we became lovers… and I actually thought that once you were out of my system I would be able to move on. Of course, out there, I finally accepted the truth. I'd fallen for a guy who couldn't love… The more I learned about you, the more I realised that.'

'I never thought I *could love* until I did…'

'It's why I handed in my resignation. I knew that was what I was going to do when I returned to London because I just couldn't envisage being in the same building as you, even if it was a couple of floors down, without my heart breaking over and over every day. Just knowing that you were only a heartbeat away, knowing that at some point I would bump into my replacement…it was too much…'

'I was a fool, my darling, but I came to my senses and I'm just glad that I did, that I finally stopped letting my past to dictate my future. Although, if I'm honest, no woman had ever captivated me the way you had…so…'

'Is there more?'

'Much more. Or maybe not *much.* But the rest is very important, the rest of what I want and need to say. Erin… I can't live without you.' He leaned into her and clasped her hands. 'I want to go to sleep with you by my side and wake up with you by my side. I want to hear your laughter every day and I'm addicted to the way you don't mind telling me what you think. You make me a better person. Erin…' He flushed and briefly looked away but then, when his eyes returned to her face, they were utterly serious. 'I never thought I would hear myself say these words with love in my heart, vulnerable and not caring that I am, but will you marry me? Be my wife? Never leave me?'

'Yes!' She smiled tenderly at him. 'After that wonderful prelude, my darling, I thought you'd never ask…'

* * * * *

Subscribe and fall in love with a Mills & Boon series today!

You'll be among the first to read stories delivered to your door monthly and enjoy great savings.

WE SIMPLY LOVE ROMANCE

MILLS & BOON SUBSCRIPTIONS

HOW TO JOIN

1

Visit our website
millsandboon.com.au/pages/print-subscriptions

2

Select your favourite series
Choose how many books. We offer monthly as well as pre-paid payment options.

3

Sit back and relax
Your books will be delivered directly to your door.